M000311968

WALKERSPIRIT

THE WALKER FAMILY ~ BOOK SEVEN

BERNADETTE MARIE

5 Prince Publishing

5 PRINCE PUBLISHING & BOOKS, LLC

PO Box 16507, Denver, CO 80216

www.5PrinceBooks.com

Digital: ISBN-13: 978-1-63112-210-1

Print: ISBN-13: 978-1-63112-211-8

WALKER SPIRIT. Bernadette Marie

Copyright Bernadette Marie 2017

Published by 5 Prince Publishing

Cover Credit: B. Soehner

First Edition 2017

5 PRINCE PUBLISHING AND BOOKS, LLC.

WALKER SPIRIT

BERNADETTE MARIE

C

P

Co

All
ma
quo
Prir

First

5 PRI

To Stan,

You continually lift my spirit
with your belief in all that I do.
I love you.

ACKNOWLEDGMENTS

To My 5: You are the spirit of my life. No matter the battle ahead of us, you are my joy.

To Mom, Dad, and Anni: Thank you for your encouragement to follow my spirit (or all 900 of them.)

Cate, thanks for putting up with my "on its own schedule" spirit. I appreciate you keeping me on track from the other side of the world.

To My Readers: Thank you for holding out for this book. It challenged me until I knew it was right.

ALSO BY BERNADETTE MARIE

THE KELLER FAMILY SERIES

The Executive's Decision

A Second Chance

Opposite Attraction

Center Stage

Lost and Found

Love Songs

Home Run

The Acceptance

The Merger

The Escape Clause

A Romance for Christmas

THE WALKER FAMILY SERIES

Walker Pride

Stargazing

Walker Bride

Wanderlust

Walker Revenge

Victory

Walker Spirit

THE MATCHMAKER SERIES

Matchmakers

Encore

Finding Hope

THE THREE MRS. MONROES TRILOGY

Amelia

Penelope

Vivian

THE ASPEN CREEK SERIES

First Kiss

Unexpected Admirer

On Thin Ice

Indomitable Spirit

THE DENVER BRIDE SERIES

Cart Before the Horse

Never Saw it Coming

Candy Kisses

ROMANTIC SUSPENSE by BERNADETTE MARIE

Chasing Shadows

WALKER SPIRIT

1

Wondering when her dress would turn to rags, and her high heels to slippers, Audrey Walker ducked out of the reception hall full of Walker family and half the state of Georgia, she reckoned. Leaned against the outside wall, she pulled off her shoes, wiggled her numb toes, and rested her head for a moment.

It had been a long day. Her aunt had been planning this ball for the past month, and it was as sweet as the one Cinderella attended, she was sure. However, Audrey had nearly single-handedly made everyone at the ball look fantastic. She'd been doing hair and make-up on everyone, in the kitchen of her condo, since early that morning. And now, as the night inched toward late, she was exhausted.

Perhaps she wouldn't ditch the night all together. After all, where else could she snap pictures on her phone of her brothers in tuxedos? She wasn't even sure Jake would wear one for his own wedding, which had also been announced at the ball.

Things were quickly changing around her, she pondered, as she heard the DJ change songs. Jake was going to marry a fellow race car driver, whom he'd always had a rivalry with. Missy

Sheridan, however, wasn't the enemy he'd made her out to be. Audrey hadn't been around Missy too much, but she thoroughly enjoyed her. She'd be happy to have Missy for a sister-in-law, and she'd fit in with the women of the Walker family. They were all bold, smart, and strong.

The wedding was planned for October. An outdoor fall wedding. And with Lydia Morgan, the owner of the reception hall and many other venues around town, in charge, it was bound to be extraordinary. Pearl, Audrey's sister who owned the bridal store and co-owned the building with Lydia, had already begun talking wedding attire with Missy.

Pearl had married Lydia Morgan's brother Tyson almost two years ago. They had eloped, though Audrey wished they'd done it up big and bold. It was a union that deserved a big celebration. They'd had a reception, but it just wasn't the same, as far as Audrey was concerned.

Perhaps their reasoning was because the Morgans had once been family rivals of the Walkers, but she couldn't say she'd ever fully bought into that. For as long as she could remember, Audrey had been friends with Lydia. And wasn't it because of Lydia that Audrey was taking the plunge into owning her own business?

With a grin on her face, she walked around to the front of the reception hall and out to the sidewalk that lined the shops in front of what her sister and Lydia had coined their *Bridal Mecca*.

The two entrepreneurial women had purchased the entire building, with hopes of filling it with businesses that were geared toward weddings. And they were certainly succeeding.

Pearl owned the bridal store. Their sister Bethany worked part-time for the florist. Her cousin Dane's fiancée, Gia, owned an Italian import gift store. Audrey had lost count of the number of businesses Lydia was involved in between venues and restaurants. She was a wonder.

Now Audrey would open her own hair salon in the same location. She wasn't sure what thrilled her more; having her own business, or being that close to her sisters every day.

The sky was dark, with no hint of the moon. But she wanted to walk to the storefront where her salon would soon be, just to be near it.

Slowly, enjoying the warmth in the air, and the sounds all around her, she walked to the dark window where a small sign said *Coming Soon! Audrey's Salon and Boutique.*

In the past week, the contractor had been working on getting the plumbing run. She'd opted for four shampoo sinks, though to start, she'd be working alone. But she didn't know if that was forever. It was better to plan ahead, she thought.

Audrey opened her tiny purse, which Pearl had loaned her with the dress, and had made her swear to return in pristine shape so she could sell it. Inside, she fished for the keys. She wanted to go inside and look around. To breathe the air in her very own space would give her a high to last for the night. She'd been in there only hours earlier, so nothing would have changed, but it did something to her to be there. Perhaps that was the same thrill Lydia got when she opened a new business. Audrey could see how it could become addictive.

Last month, when she'd walked out of the salon she'd worked at for nearly ten years, her brother Jake suggested she go into business for herself. She'd planned on buying the salon until they sold it out from under her. So she'd walked out. What else was she supposed to do? That day, she'd thought her career was over, but now, oh—the possibilities.

As she turned the key in the lock and pushed open the door, she felt that wash of pride warm her. This was what she thought of as Walker style—doing something the way you wanted to.

Everything in the salon would be right where she wanted it. The colors would be hers, the furniture, and even the magazines. How was it that she'd never thought of having something she'd built from the ground up before?

"Hi. I'm sorry to bother you, but..."

The voice of a man boomed behind her, and Audrey spun around, dropping the elegant bag to the ground and into the dust.

Her first instinct would have been to gather the bag, but she was paralyzed looking at the dark shadow of a man standing in her doorway.

"Oh, God, I didn't mean to startle you. I am so sorry." He stepped in further, and Audrey took a step back, fisting her hands at her side. The man then stood still, his hands up in surrender. "I'm just looking for Kent Black. I was told I could find him around here."

Audrey blinked hard, trying to get her eyes to focus in the dark area. "Why are you looking for Kent?" she asked. Her sister hadn't mentioned anything about someone coming for her husband. Audrey certainly wasn't going to be the person to just give up his presence.

"I'm with the film crew that's going to be making the movie here. I was supposed to be in town yesterday when they all met." She saw him shrug. "But you know, things come up."

Audrey scanned her memory for the conversation she and her sister had had that morning while she was doing her hair.

Bethany's husband, Kent Black, was a famous sci-fi novelist, and they were making a movie of his latest book. And they were doing it right in Macon, Georgia. Why, she had no idea. Bethany had told her about the hundreds of meetings Kent had had in the past few months. Then when the talent was supposed to arrive, Gregory Bishop, the actor cast in the role of the main character, called last minute and said he'd had an itch to pull some slots in Vegas.

Audrey narrowed her eyes on him trying to decide if this

man, standing in her doorway, was Gregory Bishop. If he was, she had some mixed emotions. First of all, he'd been named one of the sexiest men on the planet, or something like that. From the shape of his shadow, she could see that he easily might fit that bill. In fact, just looking at the cut of his arms where the light from outside illuminated them, those were the kind of arms that carried a woman away. She swallowed hard.

He was tall, she guessed six-four. The voice. She should recognize the voice. Because her evenings were spent with Netflix, she'd seen every Gregory Bishop movie, more than once. She'd recognized the satin sex in his voice, she thought. But as she hadn't been prepared when he spoke to her, she wouldn't have thought to single him out as the hunky movie star. She needed him to speak again.

"Kent is busy," she said, and the man nodded, running his fingers through his hair.

"Yeah, I know. On my drive from the airport to the hotel, I thought I'd better apologize. I was supposed to be here yesterday to meet with him about my character. Hollywood gets into my brain sometimes, but then I forget that people depend on me. Kent expects me to play Lieutenant Price expertly, and giving into my senseless desires sometimes gets me in trouble."

Well, that was all she needed. This was indeed Gregory Bishop standing there in front of her, having an easy conversation, and acting as if he had a conscience.

Suddenly her mind flashed to the picture of him on the cover of some tabloid at the store. She didn't have to think about what he looked like beyond just the shadowed silhouette in the doorway. She knew exactly what he looked like, and if it weren't for his reputation for being quite a playboy—oh, she'd like to trace her fingers all over those ridges that made up his chest and stomach.

But she remembered he was there looking for Kent, to apologize for being too Hollywood. She could only imagine what that meant. Maybe she'd take him to Kent after all. Kent was too good a man to have someone treat him badly. Audrey decided she wanted to see what this Gregory Bishop was all about. Her own sister had been Hollywood too. Sex, drugs, and trouble were all it brought to her. Thank God she'd moved back to Georgia, Audrey realized now. Bethany's mother had succumbed to the ills of the industry, and Bethany had begun to slide into them as well. Had it not been for Kent, who could tell where Bethany might be. Now she was a respected member of the community, married to an amazing man, and she wrote children's books. Things had worked out for Bethany. Audrey, however, wasn't so sure about a man who could drop everything for Vegas just because he was too Hollywood.

She knelt to pick up the small purse she'd dropped. Pearl was going to kill her for walking into a construction site in her borrowed dress. That, she hadn't thought about, when she decided to look at her space.

Hiking up her skirt to a modest height, she carefully walked toward the door.

"Something wrong?" Gregory asked as he stepped outside.

"My sister loaned me the dress and the purse. I dropped the purse when you startled me. And it just occurred to me that the dust from the salon floor will now be on the dress."

She watched him scan a look over her in the dimly lit doorway.

"Your sister is very picky, huh?"

"What? No. She owns the bridal shop." She pointed to the door a few down from hers. "These are samples that she hopes to sell. I can't afford to pay her for them right now, so if I mess them up..."

"I'll buy them for you," he offered. "Consider them yours."

Audrey choked out a laugh as she pulled the door closed.

"Brilliant. I'd like to put in an order for some Jimmy Choo shoes then, so I can wear the ensemble again."

"What size?"

He was toying with her, but she caught a whiff of his cologne, and as she swooned, she found she just didn't care. "Seven and a half."

"It's dark. What color is the dress?"

She locked the door and turned right into him. His hands came to her hips to steady her. Lifting her eyes up to his, she realized that Gregory Bishop was holding her, in the dark, very intimately. Was there a woman on the planet that hadn't fantasized about a moment like this?

The air seemed to stick in her lungs, and she fought for breath. Perhaps she was willing herself to faint so he'd have to administer mouth to mouth.

What in the hell was wrong with her? This man had blown off Kent's importance and came to grovel.

She stepped back, out of his ever-so-sensuous grasp. Finally inhaling, she ran her hands over the satin fabric. "Royal blue," she managed as Gregory reached out and curled a loose strand of hair around his finger.

"I love blue dresses. What's your name?"

At that moment, she wasn't sure. She blinked twice and let his voice just sink into her. "Audrey. Audrey Walker."

"Gregory Bishop," he said holding out his hand.

"I know. I mean everyone knows. Right?"

"Bethany Waterbury didn't know who I was when they cast me. We even worked together once," he said.

"Bethany is my sister."

She saw the whites of his eyes as they widened, then the grin and sparkle of his teeth in the dark. "You're Bethany Waterbury's sister?"

"Yes."

"You're not a Waterbury?"

"She's a Walker. She kept her mother's last name, as she wasn't married to my father. And because of the movie industry. Violet Waterbury, her mother, was well-known."

He nodded slowly. "It's amazing who you meet on the street."

Didn't she know it? Who would have thought she'd run into the world's sexiest man, and he'd touch her, talk to her, offer to buy her Jimmy Choo shoes.

"Ms. Walker, since you're Bethany Waterbury—forgive me—Bethany Black's sister, would you know where your brother-in-law Kent might be?" His voice was easy, sincere, and still filled with that sexy strain that was entangling her.

She let out a steady breath. "We're having a dance in the reception hall."

"Not a wedding?"

"No, just a dance. A formal dance. A ball."

"And you are you the belle of that ball?"

A laugh bubbled in her, but she refrained from letting it escape in a girlie giggle. "Do you talk to all women like this?"

He ran a finger down her cheek. "Only the beautiful ones."

Oh, he was full of crap. So why was she enjoying it so much?

"Come with me. I'll find him," she said hiking up the dress again.

"I said I'd buy you the dress," he reminded her as he followed. "You don't have to hold it and tiptoe."

"I appreciate the offer. This is better."

A moment later she felt the world slip out from under her as he scooped her up into his very muscular arms. Instinct had her wrapping her arms around his neck to hold on, and her cheek was pressed against his.

Gregory let out a chuckle. "This suits me better anyway."

"You don't need to carry me."

"I want you to wear the dress again. Maybe I could take you out somewhere nice, and you could wear it."

"I'll wear it to weddings. I have a cousin and a brother getting married this year."

"Then you can wear it three more times. I'll be here for three months. Where can I find you tomorrow at seven?" he asked.

Audrey knew she was just staring at him, but she couldn't help it. Would it be wrong to kiss the man? He probably had some Secret Service watching him. Wait, that was for the President. But wasn't the sexiest man in the world equally important?

Slowly he set her on her feet, but his hands remained around her waist.

"You haven't given me an answer yet," he prodded.

"I'm sure I'm not your type. Thank you for the lift. I'll find Kent." But she couldn't move. His hands were still on her waist, and his eyes, oh those steel blue eyes she could see now, were locked with hers. She licked her lips and watched as he bit down on his.

"I'll pick you up at seven. Where will I find you?"

Her mind was running in a million different directions. She was stupid to consider this. But it was Gregory Bishop. She'd be only a notch on his bedpost, but wouldn't that be the story to tell for the rest of her life? Nothing else in her life had ever worked out. What was one night with a famous movie star going to hurt?

"Alexander Hotel. Captain's Quarters. It's an elegant restaurant inside. You'll need a suit coat."

He smiled from one side of his mouth, and God was it sexy. "You want me to meet you there?"

"I don't know you."

Again, running his finger down her jaw, he nodded. "I'll meet you there. Wear the dress."

She wasn't sure what else to say, so she turned to find Kent. When she crossed the dance floor, she turned to see him staring at her. She was going to have to ask Pearl to extend the loan on the dress. The price tag was out of her league, but looking at the man across the room, his body sculpted by the gods, and a touch that would melt butter, she knew she wasn't going to be wearing the dress after their date—with any luck it would be in shreds on the floor of her bedroom.

2

Through the Walker grapevine, known as her brother, Audrey had heard that Kent was impressed with Gregory's apology. That didn't surprise her. Kent was probably one of the most laid back men she'd ever known. Bethany had found a winner, that was for sure.

The cool spring morning treated her to birds singing and the smell of fresh cut grass from a neighboring yard. Sitting on her patio with her brother Todd, who had opted to use her couch to sleep on after the ball, instead of driving out to the Walker ranch, which was a forty-five minute drive out of town, she sipped coffee in her pajamas. This was truly the life. Sunday mornings had always been her favorite time of the week. Sundays were a day to relax and not move, she always thought. Especially since Saturdays, for a stylist, were hell on your feet.

"You have a nice spot here, Sis," Todd observed as he looked out over the city which spread out among the treetops beyond his sister's back door.

"I love it here. I got lucky having one of my clients ready to sell at the time I was looking to buy."

"You're going to do great in your new location. Everything happens for a reason, right?" He sipped his coffee.

Todd thought like that, but she had to admit, she wasn't sure. If that was the case, then last night was one of those right place, right time things, she supposed.

She drank down her coffee, then sat with the empty mug between her hands. "Bethany called this morning and said that Gregory Bishop stayed at the ball last night after he talked to Kent."

"What a ruckus." Todd shook his head. "Yeah, he stayed. Aunt Glenda was nearly speechless. Which is what happened to most of the women. They couldn't quite grasp it." He laughed. "But for the hour he was there, he spent the time looking around as if he'd lost someone."

She felt the flush in her cheeks. "He did? Did he say who?"

"Nope," he said, but he narrowed his gaze on her. "Might have heard that he carried you into the hall though."

The smile was instantaneous. "He didn't want me lifting up my dress, afraid it would get dirty."

Todd shook his head. "I knew you were the one he was looking for. How'd you meet him?"

"He was looking for Kent, I was the lucky one he ran into. God, and those tabloid covers don't do him justice. I think he's more ripped than what you see."

Todd choked on his coffee, and coughed. "What the hell were you doing with him?"

"Just dreaming," she teased, and then lifted her coffee mug only to realize it was empty. "He's taking me out tonight."

"Don't mess this up for Kent," Todd warned and that had her straightening her back.

"Why would I do that? And what exactly is that supposed to mean?"

"It means you're not stellar in the relationship department, and he's an actor, for God's sake. Look at how messed up Bethany was when she came to live here. Do you seriously assume this guy isn't like that?"

Todd usually kept his mouth shut, unless he was one-on-one with his siblings. Even worse, he was usually right.

"Bethany cleaned up and is completely sober. She's not some Hollywood tragedy anymore."

"You're right. She's not in Hollywood at all." He sipped from his mug. "I'm just saying, this guy is still a hot topic. You said it yourself—tabloids. Kent doesn't need bad publicity because his sister-in-law is involved with the lead actor in the movie based on his book."

"I'm not involved. I'm having dinner."

"I've had dinner with a woman before, and I got involved."

"Dinner, Todd. I'm not looking for some hot affair with Mr. Hollywood." Though even as she said it, she thought of how wonderful it had felt to have her head pressed so closely to him. "I have a lot on my plate right now. I don't have time to get caught up in anything."

He sat back in his chair and finished his coffee. Todd had finally gone silent, which meant he didn't believe her. She'd call off the date, except for the fact she had no way of getting in touch with the man. So, she'd be there. She'd wear the dress and go to dinner. Nothing more could come of it.

ONCE TODD LEFT, Audrey took a leisurely walk down the path by the creek that flowed near her condo. Perhaps once summer arrived, she'd take up running again. She'd been slacking in that department. Fitness was important when you stood on your feet all day, and she felt how her body had reacted to her lazier lifestyle.

Pulling her phone from her pocket, she pressed her sister's contact photo, and waited for Pearl to answer.

"Hello." Her voice would always bring a smile to Audrey's lips. Pearl was truly her rock—her greatest supporter. Their family might be big, the Walker family, but Pearl and Audrey were tied together on both ends. Same mom. Same dad. She didn't share that same combination with any of her other siblings.

"Hey, I need to keep the dress one more day," she said and waited for Pearl to screech into the phone. She was supposed to meet her at the bridal shop at three to return it.

"Don't worry."

That wasn't the response she'd expected. "Don't worry? C'mon, I saw you eyeballing all of us all night. You were worried one of us was going to ruin your stock of sample dresses."

Pearl laughed. "No denying it. I'm not so sure Lydia didn't pop a seam dancing last night."

"I think she danced with everyone there."

"Uh-huh, everyone except Phillip Smythe."

Audrey laughed. Lydia and Phillip had a thing. He was enamored by her and she couldn't run away fast enough. "Your seamstress can fix a popped seam."

"Sure. I'm not worried. But I don't have to care about your dress," she said and Audrey slowed her pace.

"Why not?"

"It's yours. It was bought for you."

Now she stopped. "You're kidding right?"

Her sister laughed. "I'm not, but now I know it's not a joke."

"He bought the dress?"

"I can't believe you met Gregory Bishop and didn't tell me," her sister's voice rose in pitch. "God, he's gorgeous."

"It was all by accident. And he said he was going to buy me the dress, but I didn't believe him."

"Well, he's stopping by the store today to pay it off. You must have made quite an impression on him."

Audrey walked toward the bench that lined the path and sat down. "He's taking me to dinner."

Pearl laughed. "Hottest guy in America happens into our town and my sister is already dating him."

"You make me sound like a slut."

"No, I make you sound appealing. You're a catch."

"Then why haven't I found anyone yet?"

"Maybe you just did."

Now Audrey laughed. "Todd thinks there's a Hollywood type. He figures if Bethany was a mess when she arrived, this guy is one too."

"I can't say," Pearl sighed. "But he's buying you a dress, taking you to dinner, and Kent seems to like him."

"Then I'll go to dinner, and see what happens."

"Just remember, if you get to see him without his shirt on, you'd better call me."

Audrey burst out into laugher. "I'm sure Tyson appreciates me spilling those kinds of details."

"I'm female. I might be married to my own sexy cowboy, but I deserve to know."

"I'll call you. And thanks."

"For what?"

"Making me feel important."

"Oh, Audrey, you are. I'll talk to you soon."

They said their goodbyes and disconnected.

Audrey tucked the phone back into her pocket and sat there for a moment longer listening to the creek babble behind her. Gregory Bishop just happened into her life, and now she had a date.

The thought humored her, and she laughed as an older man walked by and eyeballed her.

She was tired of quick flings with clients or neighbors. She wanted what her sisters had, what her cousins had with their wives.

Standing, she tucked her hands into her pockets. It wasn't her time for that. It was a time to build her salon and move on with her life. It just so happened a very attractive and well-off man asked her to dinner. There was no need to cloud it with maybes, she decided, as she continued her walk.

But oh, it was going to be a fun ride for the night.

3

The phone call from his agent and one from his manager had been expected. Though most of the world would bow down at your feet when you'd reached his level of success, there were those few people you could count on to pull you back into reality, Gregory thought. He'd been reprimanded, scolded, and threatened. Luckily, on his own, he'd gone to Kent and talked to him. That seemed to have smoothed over a few things for his manager and agent.

And just because karma was a bitch, he expected that his mother would be calling next. The arm candy might have been a mistake, but he'd gone for the adventure, hadn't he?

He'd call his mother tomorrow, but for now, he'd send her a text and tell her he loved her. It was quickly reciprocated, so he silenced his phone and set it on the nightstand.

Picking up the remote to the TV, he clicked on Food Network and tossed the script he'd been reading to the end of the bed as he relaxed back against the pile of pillows behind him.

For the time being, he'd be living it up on the producers' dime in the suite at the Marriott, then as soon as the location for filming was secure, his trailer would be brought in, and he'd have his personal luxuries surrounding him, at least on set.

Okay, they weren't luxuries, but they were his, and that counted. It would also be nice to have his dog with him. He'd come with the trailer and his manager. For now, the ex had him, and that chapped his hide.

Sure, they'd gotten the dog when they were together, but it had always been his dog. She'd wanted some miniature yippy thing, and he'd wanted a real dog. They'd argued about it. It had even made some stupid tabloid show. He hated cell phones. Everyone everywhere could take a video of you arguing with your girlfriend, and they could sell it to the highest bidder.

He groaned as he thought of it.

He'd won out on the dog. A beautiful black lab whose dark eyes could read his soul. They'd been real original on the name too—Black Sabbath.

Okay, he'd been a shit when it came to the name. He wanted his tribute to Ozzy. She'd wanted to call him Hot Chocolate. So when he turned in the application for the dog license, got the collar, and footed the bill, he'd given him the name he wanted. What man goes by the name Hot Chocolate? He winced just thinking of it. It was bad enough he'd had to castrate the poor guy. Seriously, it had to have been some woman who came up with the idea to do that to male dogs. It felt vengeful.

As Guy Fieri tossed something into a pan, Gregory's stomach growled. He hadn't eaten since he left Vegas. Crap, that was like twenty-four hours ago. Then the thought that he was going to have dinner with the beautiful brunette came to mind, and he smiled as he rested his arm behind his head. He'd promised to meet her sister at three to pay for the dress, oh, and what a dress.

Perhaps in L.A., it would have been seen as just a casual summer dress. The thin straps and material—his chest ached at the thought of how good she'd looked in it too.

Maybe it was selfish to buy it for her—no, it was selfish. He was sure she had no idea how sexy she was in it, and hell, he was a guy who openly admitted to thinking with his anatomy and not his head.

But in those few moments he'd spent with Audrey Walker, her name seared into his brain, he'd found her delightful as well. Protective of her family, he thought. Proud of what she was building. And oh so in need of a man's attention.

Gregory turned the channel, and then again until he found the classic Batman movie with Michael Keaton, and he tossed the remote to the end of the bed with the script he'd discarded. Keaton was his favorite of all Batmans. He had that charm that Gregory thought no one else had. He strived for that in his own movies. He wanted that sex appeal to ooze off the screen.

He worked hard to chisel his body so that he looked like a real-life superhero. He fueled it to keep it that way too—well usually, he reminded himself as his stomach growled again.

Kicking his feet off the side of the bed, he stood and walked to the mini-fridge in the corner which was stocked just for him with the fruits and vegetables he'd requested. There were a few yogurts, and hard boiled eggs as well.

Gregory pulled a few items out and created himself a power meal to ease his hunger pains. He'd go down to the gym for an hour and get his workout in as well.

A smile formed on his lips as he sat down at the table by the window, which overlooked the city, and he thought of his pending date at the Alexander Hotel. She'd been very specific to be in control, he thought, as he opened the container of yogurt and gave it a stir with a plastic spoon. What could he do to make it memorable, he wondered as he took a bite. After all, he never wanted her to forget him—ever.

GREGORY DECIDED that afternoon to explore the city he was calling home for the next few months. A run to the bridal shop would be a nice way to spend his Sunday. Tomorrow, he'd be on set and the hours would be long. Today he wanted to feel normal, and enjoy the time he had.

He felt safe enough in the area to not utilize the security the producers wanted him to have. It had been a long time since he'd caused a scene anywhere. Usually, he could walk the streets and very few noticed him. He thought of it as his Marilyn Monroe charm. It was said that she could walk down the street and no one would notice her. She understood, simply, the way that average people walked and looked. It was when she turned up her sex appeal that all eyes were on her. Gregory worked on that himself. He'd admit, though, sometimes his ego got in his way. There was a reason grown men went into show business. They liked the attention—especially from women.

Today, however, he didn't want the attention. He only pined for the longing looks from a certain dark-haired beauty. The worst part was, he wasn't even sure she'd show up, after all. That would be part of this chase, he decided, and he liked it.

With his earbuds in, and Metallica thumping in his ears, he took off down the street. The spring air was fresh, and perhaps still a little crisp, but he'd warm up quickly, he thought as he quickened his pace.

There were so many more trees in the south, he thought, as he came to a stop light and waited. L.A. had its smog. Though there was a certain difference in the humidity levels, he noted.

When the light changed, he realized he was close to the quaint street where he'd met Audrey, and her sister's bridal store was close by. Slowing his pace, he jogged toward the storefront and stopped. He took his earbuds out and let them hang over the neck of his T-shirt.

The sign on the bridal shop said closed, but her sister was inside, just as she'd said she would be to meet him.

The woman behind the counter looked up. A blonde with eyes that looked right into his soul, just as his dog's eyes did. But he decided this was a protective big sister, and he could respect that. He had one of those, and he was big brother to a younger brother. There was a code.

"Good afternoon," the blonde behind the counter greeted him.

"Hi. Pearl, right?"

"Yes."

"Thanks for meeting me."

Pearl crossed her arms in front of her, a stance he'd grown accustomed to when people looked him over while they decided whether to trust him or not. "Why do you want to buy her that dress? I'd let her borrow it for another day."

He shrugged. "She looks good in it. It's not as formal where I come from. She could wear it as a casual sundress for a long time," he smiled when he saw the glimmer in her eye. "She said she has a brother getting married. What a fantastic dress for such an event."

"Again, I'd let her use it, but I assume she might be in the wedding. I don't know the plans yet. They might just get married on a race track."

"Cars?"

"Yeah."

"Cool," he said walking to the counter and leaning up against it. "Either way. I think it would be a nice gesture, and what would we have to talk about over dinner if I didn't have a story about walking into her sister's bridal shop to pay for the dress."

Pearl smiled, and he took that as a good sign. "You know, Audrey isn't very trusting."

"I gathered that when she told me she'd meet me at the restaurant."

"Sounds like her. You already know where she works and you've met her family. Making sure you don't know where she lives is her last defense I suppose."

"I think I have a lot more to learn than just that. What kind of wine does she like?"

"White."

"Flowers?"

"Tulips."

"Color?"

Pearl laughed. "I might as well give you her address."

He shook his head. "That won't help me build trust on our first date."

"First? You're planning more?"

He shrugged. "That'll depend if I impress her with the white wine and some kind of tulips."

"Pink ones. Though I'm not sure if they have them at the grocery store. Our flower shop isn't open on Sundays."

"That's a shame, but I'll figure something out."

He pulled his credit card from the band on his arm that held his phone. "Here's my card. Run it for the dress and the hand-bag. Did you lend her the shoes too?"

"Those were hers."

"She said she wanted some Jimmy Choo shoes if I were going all out."

Pearl's eyes went wide. "You're not really going to do that are you?"

"And what would I have left to buy for the second date then?"

She laughed again as she passed the charge slip toward him to sign. "You do understand that I have to warn you to take care of her, right? I have a huge family that will... I don't know what they will do to you, but don't hurt her."

Now he laughed as he took his card back from her and slipped it in the band on his arm. "I never set out to hurt people. I admit, I made dumb decisions sometimes—like stopping in Vegas when I should be here doing my job. But I try to own up to it and do it quickly. I would never hurt Audrey on purpose. So far I'm looking forward to a nice dinner. Nothing more, I promise."

"You sound sincere enough."

"You might not believe it, but I get lonely, and it's not always easy to make friends. People always want things, even if it's just to say I'm their friend. Sometimes I'd just like one that doesn't care who the hell I am."

She nodded. "You might be okay then. She's not impressed by fame. I think Bethany ruined us on thinking that anyone from Hollywood is royalty." She winced. "I'm sorry. I guess that sounds bad."

"No. I get it. I'm grateful to Bethany and Kent for the opportunity to be in this film. I'm grateful anytime I get to work."

"It's not always easy, is it?"

"I'm sure you know from Bethany, the pressure is sickening."

"She's happy out of the spotlight."

Gregory adjusted the armband and untangled his headphones. "Will you call her and let her know I took care of the dress?"

"You're not going to call her?"

"I don't have her number. I'm going to trust that she'll be at the restaurant."

"I have no doubt she'll be there, and early."

He made a mental note of that and waved as he let himself out of the store.

Replacing the earbuds in his ears, he started back toward his hotel. Maybe he'd call the Alexander Hotel, and see if they could arrange the flowers—pink tulips. This would be one of those moments where dropping his name might come in handy.

4

Pearl had called and confirmed that Audrey did indeed own the dress she was now examining in the mirror. She'd made a few adjustments since she could. Nothing big, she'd just cut out all the tags and the stupid extra pieces meant to keep it on a hanger in the store.

She'd pulled her hair up into a messy bun, which had taken her an hour to get just the way she wanted it. Her neck was bare, though she'd tried on four different necklaces.

The dress was formal, but if she downplayed it, it made the dress more casual.

On her wrist, she'd added a large band of pearls her mother had given her for graduation, years ago. With one more look, she decided it was as good as it was going to get. Now all she had to do was convince herself that this was a good idea to meet a man she didn't know at a restaurant. What did she owe him for the dress? Last night she was all but ready to pay up, no matter the price, with just one look at him. Today, however, she wouldn't sell herself that short. It was good to meet him at the restaurant. Having him not know where she lived gave her anonymity. He'd have to appreciate that, right? After all, that's why movie stars had big walls built around their houses.

Maybe it would have been better to suggest somewhere that wasn't buried in a hotel. If she could have driven by to see if he was there, wouldn't that have been better?

Then again, they could bury themselves in the restaurant, which offered private booth dining. And hadn't Todd told her that Gregory had caused a stir at her aunt's ball?

She squeezed her eyes shut. One of the things she was most skilled at was overthinking things. This was a nice dinner with a man who looked like a god. He'd bought her a dress, and he'd be in town for a few months. Nothing more would come of this than dinner.

Opening her eyes, she walked away from the mirror and headed out the door.

GREGORY WAS PLEASED with Audrey's choice of restaurants. He'd arrived early to ensure that the tulips he'd ordered had indeed been placed on the table. That's when he found out there was a Chef's Table, and he couldn't resist that.

Now he stood outside the restaurant and waited for his date. It was at that moment he realized he hadn't seen Audrey's face in the full light. Would he know her? He assumed he'd recognize the dress which he'd bought, he thought with a chuckle.

And then he saw her walking toward the hotel. There had been no doubt it was her. His heart rate ramped up the moment she crossed the street.

Gregory sucked in a breath. She'd been stunning in the dark, but in the light, she was breathtaking. He licked his lips, realizing his mouth had gone dry. What was it about this woman? Gregory had dated supermodels and Hollywood elite, but none of them had him gasping for air just by looking at them.

Audrey walked through the revolving door to the hotel, focused on tucking her keys into the small purse that went with the dress. When she lifted her head and saw him, she stopped in her tracks. For a long, silent moment, they simply stared at each other. He couldn't help but wonder if he'd had the same effect on her as she'd had on him.

He pulled in a breath and finally felt he could speak. "You look beautiful."

"Thank you. You look very handsome as well. That's a fantastic suit."

"Thank you. I have a table already." He offered his arm, but he noticed the hesitant look in her eye before she accepted it as he escorted her to their table.

When they walked back toward the kitchen, Audrey pulled back and stopped. "Where are you going?"

"Trust me," he said as he pushed open the door and led her to the table in the kitchen. "Nothing better than the Chef's Table, don't you agree?"

Her eyes had gone wide. "I didn't even know this existed."

"You're in for a treat then." He pulled out her chair and waited for her to sit before he took the other chair.

"You must have talked to my sister. I assume you had the tulips put on the table?"

He smiled. "I'm looking to impress you. Am I succeeding so far?"

"I'd better let you in on a secret. I'm not impressed with people too often. In my business, you spend your days listening to everyone's gossip and problems. It puts a chip on my shoulder."

He didn't take it personally. They probably had a lot in common when it came to being impressed by someone. But now he had a goal. "I can respect that. People are always trying to impress me, but I like genuine."

"Yes."

"I'll take that as a good sign then. We have something in common."

For the first time, he saw her smile, and he eased. He'd never been too worried about impressing someone, but it was different with Audrey. He seemed to be obsessed with her liking him.

When the chef came to the table to introduce himself, he noted the genuine smile that crossed Audrey's lips. She might have had that chip on her shoulder, but to him, it looked as though she appreciated meeting new people. Perhaps it was only him that she'd been reserved about. After all, he'd met her in a moment of weakness when he'd gone to apologize to her brother-in-law.

The chef explained the meal he was going to bring them and suggested a white wine that would pair well.

"That sounds fantastic," she said as the chef pulled the cork from the bottle.

"Would you like to sample it first?" he asked, posing his question to Gregory.

"I'm fine. Audrey?"

"I have no idea how to test a bottle of wine. I trust your judgment," she said to him, and with a nod, he poured each of them a glass. Once he was finished, he put the wine in a silver bucket of ice next to the table.

Audrey picked up her glass and looked at it. "I guess that would be fun, right? To learn about wine."

"Where do we sign up for that class? And if we start to sample wines, does that make us snobs?"

She laughed and eased back in her chair. "Aficionados," she said. "Then we could take the train through Napa Valley and try everything they had to offer."

"See, I must have impressed you somewhere. You're planning trips instead of second dates."

Now her lips pursed. "I was making conversation."

"As am I." He sipped his wine. "This is nice."

She finally took a sip of her wine. "I enjoy white wine."

Instead of telling her that he'd already known that, and talked to the chef, he simply enjoyed her watching the bustle of the kitchen.

"What made you pick this restaurant?" he asked.

"I knew I wouldn't be too dressed up. Seriously, this dress is fantastic, but it's not a dinner dress."

Gregory shrugged. "We're just from different parts of the world. It would fly in L.A."

"I don't think much of L.A. and Hollywood. I'm sure you understand."

How could he blame her? He didn't think much of it either. "Your sister?"

"She was raised in the industry. I know her mother wasn't an A-lister, but it messed her up."

"Your sister was quite successful in her own right."

"I know," she said smugly. "She's fantastic, but I'll admit it took me some time to realize that."

"She came with baggage."

"I assume you do, too."

That stung a bit, he thought, but she had every reason to consider that it was true. "You want the history?"

"We have time," she said as she picked up her wine and took, what he considered a sexy, long drink.

Before he could begin, the chef brought an appetizer to the table. He explained the simple Caprese skewers that he brought to start them.

Audrey picked one up and bit the tomato from the bottom, sliding it from the skewer with her teeth. He was sure she hadn't meant to drip the simple motion with sex, but he had to bite the inside of his cheek to keep his mouth from falling open.

Talking might offer him an out, he thought, as he watched her with great enjoyment. "I'm from Nebraska. Cornhusker fan all the way." He waited for a reaction, but she suppressed it if she had one. "Anyway, Dad is a farmer. He met Mom in college. She was from San Francisco and couldn't quite hack the farm wife role. When they divorced, she took my brother, sister, and me back to California with her."

"How'd you get into acting?"

"Sophomore year of high school I got the lead in Camelot."

She narrowed her eyes. "Which lead. Camelot has two distinct male leads."

He couldn't help but smile now. "You know your stuff. I'd like to say I was Lancelot. Everyone thinks Lancelot and assumes stud."

"King Arthur?"

"To this day, best role I've ever had. On the stage that is."

"As a sophomore?"

He laughed. "Oh, it pissed off a lot of people."

"So you sing?"

"I can hold a note."

She sipped her wine again, and then licked her lips. Perhaps she was playing him now. "One lead in a high school musical doesn't get you into movies."

He shrugged. "Sometimes it does. My junior year, my uncle came to see our piss-poor production of Les Miserables. My rendition of Jean Valjean won him over. He was casting for a show about some high school band. It was aimed at middle school viewers. We ran for three seasons."

Audrey's eyes went wide. "Our High School Band?"

He laughed. "You remember the show?"

"It was horrible," she said with such sincerity that he laughed aloud and even the kitchen crew sent him glances.

"That's honest."

Her cheeks flushed with color. "I'm sorry. I'm sure you worked hard on it."

"We did. We busted our asses for them." Deciding it would be easier to hold a conversation if they were closer, he picked up his wine and moved to the chair next to her. "I fell in love with Tasha McAllister."

"The blonde drummer?"

"You do remember the show. If only we'd had a few million true followers like you," he joked. "But yeah. She was my first true love."

"What happened to her?"

"Overdosed at twenty-one."

Audrey tossed her hands in the air. "And you wonder why I'm not sold on Hollywood types?"

Gregory nodded. "I've never done a drug in my life."

"I'm supposed to believe that?"

"I'll have a glass of wine. I'll throw back a few beers. But I'll do yoga for a headache before I take a Motrin. I see it every day. Pop this, down that. I may not grace movie posters or the front pages of tabloids my whole life. But wouldn't it be good to be still alive and do something else?"

Her shoulders eased. "Bethany was addicted to prescription meds. So was her mother."

He nodded. "I remember her mother's death. That's the tragic side." He decided the conversation was taking a drastic downturn, so he changed the tone. "I'm still a Cornhuskers fan, and I make it to Nebraska for harvest every year."

The flash in her eyes said she knew what he was doing. "You blew off the first reading of the movie you're in now for a night in Vegas. That must have been fairly important to you."

Ah, but she wasn't done raking him over the coals. Well, he thought, he'd oblige her. "I did. Privilege gets me in trouble, but not drugs."

Audrey tucked a loose strand of hair behind her ear. "Did you at least win while you were in Vegas?" She smiled when she asked.

"Lost two grand at craps, won it back in blackjack."

"So you're a gambling man?"

"I gambled on a dress and won a dinner date."

She leaned in closer to him. "This might be the only date you get out of me."

"I don't doubt it. But don't tell me you're ready to run out yet. I promise I'll be too busy with the movie next week to bother you too much."

Audrey considered for a moment. "I'll stay for dinner. You fascinate me, but I'm not sold."

Gregory was a man on a mission he decided at that moment. She'd be sold by the time they wrapped up in Georgia. He'd bet on it.

5

Audrey would have to admit that the dinner at the Chef's Table was spectacular. She'd never quite had an experience like that. Usually, she'd like to have control over what she ate, but there was something fascinating about food being brought to the table.

She ate items she might not have chosen to try on the menu. There was a texture issue when it came to eating clams, but at least Gregory hadn't laughed when she gagged. He simply finished the clams.

Now he walked her to the car, and his hands were tucked safely in his pockets, she noted. That was fine. This was a one-time thing, and something she could brag about to her friends down the line. After all, he was the sexiest man in the world, according to the tabloids. She, on the other hand, was just a hair stylist trying to build something for herself. Their worlds were not compatible, nor were they probably going to cross paths again.

Audrey pulled the key fob from her purse and unlocked her car. As she opened the door, she turned to Gregory. "Thank you for the nice evening, and for the dress. It was fun to play dress-up and go out."

"You're very welcome," he replied as she started to climb into her car. "Wait."

Audrey stopped and stood to look at him.

"I'd like to take you out again if you'd consider it."

She worried her lip a moment. "You want to go out with me again?"

"I would."

"I'm just a hair stylist from Macon, Georgia. Are you sure you want to waste your time on me?"

Gregory took a step closer, his hands still in his pockets. "It's not wasting my time. I'm intrigued by you, and I'd like to spend a little more time with you."

What was she getting herself into? She was fairly sure it was the lead-up to heartbreak, but she couldn't help herself. Looking into those dark eyes, she got a bit lost.

"Okay. I'll accept your offer. But when will you have time?"

"I'll call you. I have read-throughs tomorrow, so I'm unsure of my schedule."

That she expected. Even though she'd accepted his invitation, she was sure that it would take a bit more work to get together. Maybe she wouldn't see him again after all, but she'd let him think they would.

"Give me your phone," she instructed. He pulled it from his pocket, unlocked it, and handed it to her. "You're not afraid that I'll see something you don't want me to?"

"Swipe left and right. I have nothing to hide," he offered, and his eyes were sincere.

Maybe he was straight up, just as he'd said he was at dinner.

Audrey typed her phone number into the contacts and then took a photo of herself and added it to the contact. It made her giggle to herself, and she noticed his grin.

"Okay, you can get a hold of me now," she told him as she handed him back his phone. "I won't hold you to it. I know you're going to be busy, and I know I'm not your type."

He gave her a slow, thoughtful nod as he replaced his phone in his pocket. "Oh, don't assume anything. Obviously, I've never found a woman that was my type, or I suppose I'd be taken. I guess I'm still trying to figure out my type. You just might be it." He took her hand, lifted it to his lips, and placed a kiss on it. "Thank you, Audrey. I had a delightful evening. I'll be talking to you soon."

She wasn't sure where the shift happened, but she wanted to pull him in and kiss him senseless. However, she refrained. Instead, she slid into her car and started the engine as he shut the door. Then he stepped away as she pulled from the curb.

GREGORY WATCHED HER DRIVE AWAY, and he cursed his blessed life. It was one thing to have everything you ever wanted, and another to have people judge you for it.

He walked back to the hotel where he'd valeted his car. Handing the attendant his slip, he pulled out his phone while he waited for them to retrieve his car.

Opening the contacts to Audrey's photo, he smiled down at it. So maybe she had a reason for not wanting to get involved with an actor. His first impression couldn't have been well received, after all, he'd stood up the production crew, and that never went over well. But then there was Bethany. She'd been a good actress, he remembered, but he'd never seen her in anything that wasn't a B-horror film. At least he didn't think he had. And when they had worked together, years ago on one of those horrible horror movies, she hadn't even looked his way.

Hollywood changed people. A dye job here, a boob job there. Most actors weren't even recognized from their first films.

Drugs ran rampant in the industry. Sometimes it started out innocently enough... just to get enough energy to finish a damn film. Other times it was to control body weight or curb anxiety. But it had taken a toll on Bethany and her mother. Obviously, it strained her relationships with her siblings too.

As he watched them pull his car into the drive, he took a few dollars from his pocket, handed it to the attendant, and drove away from the hotel.

There was much more to Gregory Bishop than what the tabloids crowned him. Sure, he'd fallen into what they'd made him out to be too many times. Cell phones were a bitch when it came to making mistakes. Anyone and everyone had no problem taking video of you on a date, having one too many glasses of wine or, God forbid, that moment you take your best friend's wife out the side door while he picked up the tab. Yeah, that had been a bitch to recover from. But it was the way it worked. Now here he was in an unglamorous town in middle Georgia, and he wished for peace from the life that he'd grown accustomed to.

As he drove toward his hotel, he wondered what it was that would make someone like Audrey see him differently? He wasn't just about memorizing some lines and wearing a costume. There was more to him. He was fairly handy with tools. That had been instilled in him on the farm. Maybe on his off time, he could help her put her salon together. There was great pride in that for Audrey, and he'd like to be part of it.

He was willing to understand reluctance to commitment on her part toward him. He'd only be there for a short time, but he'd like to be a useful member of the community in that time. Maybe that was what he should strive for no matter the location he was filming. His father would be proud of that.

Finally, a wave of pride moved through him as he pulled into the valet at his hotel. For the first time in a long time, he felt as though he had a purpose and it felt good.

6

Since the salon Audrey used to work at was closed on Mondays, she didn't have many Monday clients. It had been a long time since she'd worked Mondays and she wasn't sure if she wanted to start that up again. It was nice to have two days off in a row, she thought.

But since she didn't have any clients heading to her house for appointments, she woke early, walked down to the coffee shop to get her exercise and her breakfast, and then headed to her new salon to get some grunt work done. Her cousin, Russell, was going to meet her there and put in a few hours tiling the back room floor.

When she pulled up, he was standing out front with a huge mug of coffee and his sunglasses on. "If I didn't know better, I'd have thought you pulled an all-nighter," she said as she climbed from her car.

"I have a three-year-old who wants to sleep in our bed all night with his foot up my ass, and an uncomfortable, pregnant wife. And I'm afraid if she's this uncomfortable now, she's going to be miserable when she gets bigger."

Audrey smiled as she took her keys from her bag and

unlocked the door. "Her little tummy is precious. Though she does look further along than Susan, and I thought they were due about the same time."

"They are. Everyone is different."

"As long as she's healthy," she offered, as she pushed open the door. "They delivered all of the supplies on Friday. It's in the back. The plumber will be here today too, and I'm going to be working on painting the treatment room."

"What the hell is a treatment room? Or do I even want to know?"

She snorted out a laugh. "Waxing, facials, and massage. Things I can guarantee your wife would love to have done now, while she's pregnant, and again after the baby is born."

"I'll keep that in mind. It sounds like we all have our work cut out for us," he said as he pulled off his sunglasses and tucked them into the collar of his shirt. "I hear you had a date yesterday."

Audrey blew out a breath. "Seriously? This is what everyone has to talk about?"

Russell shrugged. "I suppose if it was just Dave from the coffee shop we might not wag our tongues as much. But since the very name Gregory Bishop makes my wife swoon, it's a bigger deal."

"That doesn't make you mad?"

He chuckled. "I knocked her up and I wear her ring," he offered as he lifted his left hand. "No need to get mad. So, is he a nice guy? I mean he did miss his first day of work. He doesn't sound upstanding."

Audrey crossed her arms in front of her. "He did miss it. But he came directly to Kent and apologized. And to answer your question, he's a very nice man. His roots don't differ too much from yours. He's a farm boy."

"No kidding?" he asked with a nod. "Well, that's something. We're a good breed of people."

"Get started on the floor," she ordered playfully as she set her bag on the work table in the center of the room. "I'm going to go talk to Pearl for a moment."

"She's not open for another hour."

"Oh, if I know my sister, she's already been at work for an hour setting up."

Audrey was right. Pearl was happily moving about her store organizing and personalizing the displays for brides who had appointments. Audrey tapped on the front door, and her sister's head shot up, then a smile formed when she saw her standing there.

Pearl hurried to the door and pulled it open. "You have no idea how exciting it is to me that you're going to be next door all the time and can drop in."

"You'll get tired of me," Audrey assured her as she stepped into the shop and Pearl locked the door behind her before pulling her into a hug. "Ah, you're in a sappy mood this morning. What's up?"

"I went to Mom's last night."

And that said a lot, Audrey thought. Pearl and their mother didn't always see eye to eye, and usually, after a meeting, Pearl needed Audrey more. So she settled into the role of supportive sister.

"How is she?"

The smile faded from Pearl's face. "She's Mom. Miserable. The world is hard. Still stuck on Dad, for what reason I can't even imagine. She knows he has some sugar mama and it makes her mad."

"I wish she'd get over it. He wasn't worth it thirty years ago, and he's not worth it now."

"She's on my ass to have kids, and then turns around and

says that if she's a grandmother she'd be old, and she cries. Tyson and I are happy right where we are for now. I don't want her pushing."

Audrey couldn't help but wonder how her sister and her husband managed with the families they had. Tyson Morgan had been raised by his grandfather, and he was a hard-ass man. The rest of Tyson's story was simply sad, she thought. His birth mother abandoned him, and he was raised to think his uncle, who had died, was his father. Her head spun when she thought of the soap opera that was his life.

It had only been recently that the Morgans and the Walkers had fallen into a kind relationship with one another, though Tyson's sister Lydia had always been a friend to Audrey.

Now Tyson Morgan was married to Audrey's sister, whose own family had never been close. But they were making it work, and each day, their side of the Walker family grew closer and closer.

Pearl picked up her coffee mug and took a long sip. The pearls on her wrist shifting, bringing the attention to her elegant nails and the perfect manicure. She was absolute class, Audrey thought as she watched her.

"So how are things going in your salon?"

"The plumber is on his way, and Russell is doing some tile work. I am going to do some painting in the treatment room." She smiled. It would be nice to offer more than just hair in her salon. The possibilities were endless. "I think in the next month we will be completely ready."

"Good. You don't have any clients this morning?"

"Not today."

"Perfect," she said moving from behind the counter. "My first bride isn't due for another hour. Let me get more coffee, and you can tell me all about your date with Gregory Bishop," Pearl sweetly demanded as she walked back toward the small kitchen area in her store.

Audrey dropped her shoulders and let out a disapproving grunt. There simply wasn't anything to tell, but she followed Pearl, remembering the night in her head. The very thought that he wanted to see her again brought a warmth to her cheeks.

She pushed it from her mind as she sat down at the small table in the room while Pearl pressed the button on the coffee maker to brew a single cup of coffee.

If she even let herself think she wanted another moment with Gregory, she'd be letting herself down. She knew that. They came from different worlds and didn't have anything in common. But the thoughts kept circling in her head. What if she were his type? What kind of life would they have then?

7

Gregory was early. Sadly, he was used to kissing ass to get back on the good side of producers and directors.

Sure, they'd brown-nose him if he played that card. He was the talent they'd sought out. The audition for Lieutenant Price had been a formality. There was no doubt in his mind the same had happened when casting his female lead, Sherri Post. She was cast to be the looker in the film, though he thought he could hold that on his own.

Sherri was the buxom blonde with the implants that seemed to sell sci-fi pictures when her uniform was a bit tight. Gregory shook his head at the thought. What happened to good 'ole science fiction? Robots, spaceships, and discovering new planets and new species used to be enough. Okay, that was a lie too. Hollywood was built on the sexuality of the leading woman, and the striking good looks of the leading man.

He chuckled to himself as he walked into the room at the hotel where they'd be running through the script before taking a tour of the warehouse that housed the set. The only reason to film a movie of this caliber in Georgia was that the production was getting some fine kickbacks from the city. They'd get the publicity, and the producers were saving some money. What did he care? He was happy to be steadily employed. And if it hadn't been a Kent Black book, he'd never have met Audrey Walker. Wasn't fate a funny thing?

Gregory found his chair by the paper plaque with his name on it. There was a bottle of his favorite water because he'd come to realize everything like that mattered to the talent, really even when it didn't. He could care less if they'd served him a glass of tap water, but agents weren't paid to make sure you had tap water. They were paid to make sure the talent was happy, comfy, and employed. All perks, he thought.

He sat down in the chair and thumbed through the script, which he already knew. There was more to being the talent than being sexy and handsome. They expected him to do a good job if he was going to be steadily employed, and hadn't he already tested that?

There was no pride in being a prick, he knew. And he was still waiting for that phone call from his mother to tell him as much. It only meant she hadn't caught wind of it yet. She usually was privy to the information quickly. That's what happened when your big break as a sixteen-year-old came at the hands of an uncle who happened to be in the business. He called home about everything.

Though that uncle had long ago retired he still had connections. One of those connections happened to be with Gregory's current manager.

Gregory looked up from his script when he heard another person walk into the room. He wasn't surprised when Kent Black walked in, his laptop and script held protectively to his chest as he balanced a cup of coffee in one hand and tried to gain control of his bag which was slung across him, and winning the battle to be front and center.

"Mr. Bishop, hi. Hello. Good morning," Kent stammered as he looked for his name.

"I think you're right there," Gregory pointed as he stood and moved to Kent. "Let me help you with all of that."

He reached for the coffee first, allowing Kent to free his hand and lay down the laptop and script before they crashed to the floor. Removing his bag from his body, Kent hung it on the back of the chair.

"Thank you. My wife says I'm a tad bit unorganized. Says it's my creativity, but that's what she loves about me," he laughed.

"Your creativity is genius. We should all be helping you out. Without your words, we wouldn't be here to work."

Kent smiled, then pushed back his hair. "I appreciate that."

He opened his laptop as Gregory walked back to his seat. "I'm sorry again for missing the first read-through. Very unprofessional of me."

"I suppose you need a break once in a while."

"Doesn't mean vanity should be a reason to be a jerk." Gregory sat down and opened the special bottle of water. "I know I apologized already, but I'm hoping it'll leave a good mark for me. I'm trying to make a good impression on your sister-in-law."

Kent's head rose at that, and his brows drew together. "Audrey?"

"Yes."

"Well, she's a sweet girl."

"She's not too sold on me yet," he admitted. "She doesn't seem to be impressed with status—nor should she be."

"Of course they're all a little biased about that. My wife had a hard start in her life. They see the entertainment industry a little differently than others might."

"Understood. When does Audrey plan to open her salon?"

Kent scratched the back of his neck and shrugged. "I don't

know really. I've been so caught up with this production that I haven't paid a lot of attention. I know that their cousin Russell is helping with the construction. He was in a horrible accident last year, and this is a great recovery for him."

"They sure do have a sense of family, don't they?"

Kent chuckled as he sat down. "They do. The Walkers are very close. Audrey and my wife are extremely close to their siblings since they have a uniquely broken home," he said just as others began to filter into the room.

Gregory rose to greet those who had joined them, but what Kent had just said still danced around in his head. Uniquely broken home. He was from a broken home, but there was nothing unique about it, he thought as he sat back down and sipped from his water again.

He wouldn't pry any more with Kent, who seemed to be even more frazzled now that the room had filled. This was a conversation to have with Audrey, face to face. Maybe over a bottle of wine—or champagne. Yeah, that was better. They could do a little celebrating of her new location—her new beginning.

Gregory smiled as he watched the others take their seats. To new beginnings.

8

By the time Audrey was finished painting the treatment room, she was dizzy. How did painters do it, she wondered. The fumes were horrible. That made her laugh. People often walked into salons, and that was the first thing they'd bitch about.

It had gotten better over the years, that was for sure. But between permanents, hair colors, artificial nail services and then the fragrance usually added to the ambiance to cover up those smells—it was a lot.

Audrey didn't do too many perms anymore. The hair color she used had very little odor. And she'd long ago gone to doing natural nail services and gels, which emitted very little smell.

She figured her sister would appreciate that. What bride wants to be trying on dresses and gagging on salon smell.

For a while there would be new construction smell though, but that mean new beginnings. What a wonderful feeling—new beginnings. The day she'd walked out of the other salon, she couldn't have imagined anything would ever go right for her again. But here she was, building something that was all hers.

Pride swelled in her chest. Perhaps that was fate taking over that day. There was one opening in the *Bridal Mecca* building, which her sister quickly earmarked for her. Looking around, she thought it would be a place people would tell their friends about. Those bridal parties would book their days with her now. She was part of something bigger.

Russell walked through the front door with two bottles of water in his hands. "I raided Lydia's office fridge. She's got some flavored waters in there too. She said to help yourself if you'd like."

Audrey smiled as she took the water he handed her. "I suppose I should think about those things. Coffee maker, fridge, water, tea." She laughed. "This is going to be great, isn't it?"

"I think so. Come look at the tile. See what you think," he said as he opened his water and took a sip.

Audrey followed him to the back room and stopped when she saw the beautiful faux wood tiles gleaming up at her. "Oh, Russ. This is fantastic."

"It is." He chuckled. "It looks nice and will stand up to everything. When your plumber gets everything else roughed in, we can start planning for the main room. Are you carpeting the waiting area?"

"Area rug. This tile will run everywhere."

He nodded. "I might bring in Gerald to help," he said of his other brother. "We'll get you set and on your way. Are you having a grand opening party?"

Audrey instinctively shrugged. "I don't know. I hadn't thought about it."

Russell chuckled again. "Lydia has thought about it. She was asking me. She's the right gal to make it happen. Susan could cater. Bethany could deck the place out in flowers. Pearl will build you a clientele from her shop."

"I have a clientele."

"Well, then she'll add to it. Are you going to hire others?"

"Eventually. But they have to be the right people. I'm in no hurry."

He smiled. "I'm proud of you. It's going to be great."

She nodded. It sure was.

Russell cleaned up and headed home to his family. Audrey continued her painting in the bathroom, which would be a matte gray with a waterfall faucet into a glass bowl sink. Her brother, Jake, had picked it out. He had a way of transforming spaces and making them elegant. His house was proof of that.

Audrey poured paint into the tray just as she heard a dog barking, and it sounded as if it were barking in her salon. She put down the can, grabbed a rag, and hurried out to the main room as she wiped her hands.

Standing in the doorway was the sexy Hollywood god, and, she assumed, his dog.

"Hi," she said, as she eased toward the door. "You got a dog?"

"He's mine. He just arrived, as did my trailer."

"Your trailer?" she asked as she set the rag on the makeshift work table in the center of the room.

"It's on set with me. When you spend fourteen hours a day somewhere, you need something of your own."

She nodded. "And you came here why?"

"He wanted to meet you. I told him all about you."

Narrowing her eyes, she slid him a smile—careful to keep it minimal. "I'll bet you did," she smirked as she held her hands out to the dog, who sniffed her before she ran her hands over his dark, beautiful coat. "Oh, he's very sweet."

"He's a little wound up from the travel."

Audrey knelt down in front of him and continued to rub the dog into a blissful state. "What's his name?"

"Black Sabbath."

She laughed. "Black Sabbath?"

"Eh, it was a jab at the ex. She wanted some sissy name, and I wanted a tribute to Ozzy. I got my way. What would you have named him?"

"I've never had a dog."

"Who grows up without a dog?"

She scratched Black Sabbath behind the ears. "People whose mothers move around too much. We never had the yard for a dog."

He watched her stand, and Black Sabbath nuzzled her leg with his nose. "I thought the Walkers owned some huge ranch."

"You'd be correct. But my father was never much a part of that. At least he didn't work the land like my uncle and his sons. Our side of the Walker family lived in town. And it was only my sister Pearl and I, with our mom."

Gregory eased against the doorjamb and settled his eyes right on hers. "You have a story, don't you?"

"Don't we all?"

"You wouldn't want to take a walk with us, would you? There has to be a nice walking path or something around here."

Audrey bit down on her bottom lip. "I have things to do. Besides, I thought you were busy this week."

"Got done early." He gave a nod toward the sidewalk. "Less than an hour. I promise."

Why was this man interested in spending time with her? They'd just met. He was far out of her league, yet he seemed enthralled by her—her, of all people. Certainly, she was the least interesting person, and he'd soon find that out, she thought. But what would it hurt to take a walk with a gorgeous dog and his owner?

The thought had her laughing, and Gregory cocked his head.

"What's so funny?"

"Nothing at all. Let me get my phone and my keys. You promise, less than an hour?"

"Promise."

Audrey retrieved her keys and phone, then locked the door to the salon as she walked out with Gregory and Black Sabbath.

"Which way?" he asked.

"Let's go this way. There's a fantastic trail that goes down by the river."

"Sounds nice."

Audrey started down the street. The dog between her and the man.

He had some anonymity here, she noticed, as people passed right by him. Obviously, they were not yet aware of what was going on in town. It wouldn't last, she was sure. Once people realized the movie was being filmed there, and that the stars were walking freely on the street, there'd be some attention. By then she'd be long forgotten. All the better. In all honesty, she didn't have time for these kinds of distractions.

9

A spring breeze accompanied them on their short walk toward the trail by the river Audrey had mentioned. Gregory liked the quaint area, quite a bit. It was only a few blocks long, perhaps what some areas called an *Olde Town* which had been revamped with new businesses in remodeled buildings.

The building that would house Audrey's salon was being built into a bridal location. He didn't have to look it up on the internet to notice that. But he had. In the past year they had taken the building, owned by Lydia Morgan and Pearl Walker-Morgan, and completely revamped it as the all-in-one *Bridal Mecca*—which it was called.

Gregory thought they were absolute geniuses, these women with their combined talents. He and his brother and sister didn't have much in common when it came to their talents. He was envious of the bond.

"I promised I'd get you back in an hour, but I was hoping you'd at least talk to me while we walked," he said when he realized that they'd walked nearly three blocks without speaking.

"I'm sorry. I guess my head is somewhere else," she admitted and slowed her gait.

"Do you walk this path a lot?"

Audrey shifted her head in his direction. "Quite often."

"So you must live nearby."

He saw the twitch of her lips before she pursed them. "Not too far."

Fine, he'd save that for another conversation. "So tell me about your family. About your brothers and sisters."

Audrey laced her hands in front of her, then lifted them over her head as if doing a stretch. Maybe she was limbering up to run, he thought.

"Why do you want to know about them?"

"I want to know about you. I thought it was a good place to start a conversation."

She let out a long breath and lowered her arms. "I've already told you quite a bit about Bethany."

"I know she's your half-sister. I know that she was an actress and is now married to the greatest author ever."

That brought a smile to her face. "I don't read a lot of sci-fi."

"You should."

"I've read his. I just didn't realize he was the greatest author ever."

Now he smiled. "Now you know."

She nodded, and now swung her arms as they walked down a small incline that took them next to the river. "My family," she started. "My sister and I are the product of one of my father's marriages. My brothers Jake and Todd are from another. Bethany is from a relationship that didn't end in marriage."

"I'm going to take it, from your sarcastic tone, that you're not close to your father."

"None of us are really. He does things his own way. You know about Violet Waterbury, Bethany's mom. She was unique. My brothers's mother is, well, weak and whiny?" She shrugged. "I don't mean that as her personality is bad, she's just..."

"Weak and whiny?"

She laughed, and oh, he was beginning to enjoy that laugh a lot.

"Yeah. My mom is a diva on a budget."

"Wants, wants, wants and can't have."

Her pace slowed. "Yes. I suppose I just appease, but Pearl tries to be the good daughter. Unfortunately, she's usually disappointed when she tries. Nothing is good enough."

"But the five of you are close?"

"Inseparable. We have to be. The four of us have always been tight. Bethany was someone that just happened to be related if you will."

"So your relationship with her is new?"

He noticed she checked her watch before she continued. "She moved out here after her mother's death. About the time my grandfather passed. But we've all become very close, and that includes her."

"I think that's a wonderful thing. What about the other side of the Walker family?"

"My cousins?"

"Yeah."

"They're all tight-knit. All five of them. Hard-working men who are strong-willed, and love their mama."

"As it should be."

"Yeah," she sighed. "As it should be."

Well, he'd taken her down a road she wasn't too happy to wander, he figured. Her expression had waned, and her pace slowed.

"How long have you worked in a salon?"

She began to stretch again. Maybe that was a ritual as she walked.

"Since I was nineteen. So, forever."

He chuckled, thinking that didn't lead him to find out how old she was, but he figured they were close in age. Another question for another time—and there would be another time.

Shifting her head, she looked up at him. "Tell me about your brother and sister. I know your parents are divorced."

So she'd paid attention. He'd say that was a win.

"My brother, Scott, is married with three kids. Lives not far from my mother in Oakland. My sister, Kate, is stationed in Japan right now."

"Military wife?"

"No, military surgeon."

A smile lit her face. "No kidding?"

"Pretty impressive, huh?"

"Yeah." The word sighed from her lips, and the smile remained. "I love strong women. Statement makers."

"Like you?"

Now she laughed. "Oh, I'm no statement maker."

"I disagree," he said, and that's when she stopped walking.

"You don't know me," she said coolly as Black Sabbath yanked on the leash to continue their walk.

"I know enough. You're strong. Powerful. Beautiful."

The smile disappeared, and she bit down on her lip. "Why do want to spend time with me?"

"I'm new to town," he joked, but she didn't laugh now. "I'm interested."

"In me?"

On a whim, mostly to see how she'd react, he reached his hand to her cheek. When she didn't pull away, he figured that was another win. "In you, Audrey Walker. I've been interested since the moment you turned around in the dark in your salon."

Lifting her hand, she rested it on his but didn't pull back. "I haven't been in a relationship in years. I'm not good at them.

Until my siblings began to get married, I didn't think it was possible for our family to know what a stable relationship looked like. The interest I understand." She swallowed hard and stepped in closer to him. "I'm interested too."

"Then we don't have a problem."

"You don't belong here," she said.

Gregory dropped his hand from her cheek to her shoulder as the dog nudged his leg. "So this is the end of this?" he asked as he let his hand slide down her arm and capture her hand. "You're not curious to find out where interest takes us?"

"You're here for a few months. Then what?"

"I don't know. But you're right. I'm here for a few months, and Audrey, I'd really like to get to know you in that time."

He stepped closer to her, the dog now wrapping himself around their legs with his leash. When her lips parted, as though she wanted to say something, he moved in and took her mouth with his.

A gasp escaped her throat, but she didn't pull back. In fact, he was pleasantly surprised to find her hands come up between them and rest on his chest.

With his free hand, he rested it on her hip and moved her in even closer.

Need, want, curiosity all filled the warmth of her lips pressed against his. Her tongue moved against his. It was wild, new, and damned sexy.

When she lifted her arms around his neck, he knew she'd tumbled into a new feeling she might not have been welcoming, but it was there. He pressed his hand to the center of her back and kept her close. Nothing else around them mattered as long as her mouth worked against his.

When Black Sabbath yanked against the leash, which was now fully wrapped around them, he pulled back and laughed. "I think he wants to move on."

"Me too," she said with her voice airy and dripping with the sexual need he could only assume they both felt burning between them.

"Let's keep walking," Gregory offered, his voice unsteady.

Once they untangled themselves, and Black Sabbath took the lead down the path, he reached for her hand and linked their fingers. He watched her suck in a breath, but she kept her hand in his. Something new was in the making. He liked thinking of it as a new adventure, and he craved adventure. What better place to have one than in Georgia?

10

Audrey swept the floor of her kitchen before her next client was due. She hated doing hair in her house. If she had a place for it, that would be one thing, but in the kitchen—yuck.

The plumber had called her an hour ago and let her know that the inspections were complete. It was time to finish the floor. She'd called Russell, and he'd promised that he and Gerald would get started on that tomorrow.

Sitting down at her desk, in the spare bedroom that she called an office, she looked at the shipping information for her equipment. Everything was due to arrive the following Monday. She had a week to get everything done in the space, and it was going right on schedule.

Having worked on an hourly schedule, as she had for so many years, she appreciated timelines. Nothing was worse than getting behind.

When the doorbell rang, Audrey looked at her watch. She had a half hour before her next client.

She hurried to the door to answer, and when she did, she was met with the biggest arrangement of roses she'd ever seen.

"Ms. Walker?" The male voice asked from behind the flowers.

"Yes."

"These are for you," he said as he handed them to her and now his young face was exposed. "I need you to sign for them." He held out a clipboard, and she signed the sheet as he held the board steady. "Have a nice day," he offered, as he turned and hurried back to his van.

She could feel her cheeks flush with heat, alone in her own home.

Kicking the door closed, she walked to the coffee table and set down the flowers. The card was buried among the long-stemmed, fragrant beauties. *I was thinking about you. G-*

Her heart slammed in her chest, and she wanted to cry. No one bought her flowers. Bethany would give them to her once in a while from the shop. Or her brothers would send them if she was down, and they knew that would cheer her up. But a man—her head spun and she sat down on the sofa. A man she'd just met, kissed—oh, the delight of the moment was nearly overwhelming.

She reached for her phone only to realize that she'd given him her number, but she didn't have his.

Well, it was up to him then, she decided. Then it struck her that she'd never told him where she lived.

Scrolling through her phone, she texted Kent.

Did you give Gregory my address?

She looked through Facebook as she waited for a reply.

No. He asked me to call the florist he bought them from and give it to them. Wants to wait 'til you invite him over. Not a stalker.

Laughter rolled through her as she read the text. Well then, he might be the most honest man to come out of Hollywood yet.

Because it intrigued her, she brought up the IMDb app on her phone and searched for Gregory Bishop.

If there was any perk to *seeing* someone famous, it was that when she missed his face, she need only look him up online and there he would be. Of course, since the first eighteen photos of him were with sexy, elegant women, she'd have to look past that. A few, she recognized as co-stars in his movies. But there was one... A luscious redhead with an amazingly toned body and long, long legs.

Audrey took in a long breath. She knew this was the ex, since one of the photos also had Black Sabbath in it. This was where she needed to hoist up those big girl panties and keep that ex part in mind. She also had to keep in mind that she knew it was an ex because she'd heard about it on TV.

Considering that the fragrance from the roses was filling up the room, and she'd been the one kissing him yesterday, it was a bit easier to remember. But it mixed very heavily with the shouldn't-expect-too-much part too.

This time when the doorbell rang she moved to it, her professionalism already taking over. "Hey, Starla, how are you today?"

The forty-something, a mother of three, smiled at her. "I'm so grateful you are taking clients. I'm a mess," she said. Her voice dripping in southern drawl.

"Happy to do it. Your next appointment will be at my new salon," she offered, as she began to escort her client to the kitchen.

"Oh, my, Lord." Starla stopped as they walked through the living room. "Who sent you such a bouquet? Those are absolutely breathtaking."

And it begins, Audrey thought. "I met a guy. It's not serious," she quickly added.

"He wants it to be."

"Why would you say that?"

"An arrangement like that would cost a couple of hundred dollars. He must like you an awful lot."

Audrey's breath caught in her chest. "Maybe he had a Groupon," she quipped, and that brought a roll of laughter from Starla as they walked into the kitchen.

As she set Starla in a chair and covered her with a cape, she thought about what she'd said. A couple of hundred dollars. It was already too deep, she argued with herself. A dress, a fine dinner, and the roses. She could hardly breathe. It had already gone too far.

GREGORY STOOD LOOKING at himself in the full-length mirror as the final pieces were added to his uniform.

"Stunning," he said at his reflection. "Futuristic military does me good." He laughed as the woman adjusted his jacket. "Hey, Kent," he called out, as Gregory saw him walk in.

"It will never cease to amaze me that they can reproduce what I have in my head."

"Nice, huh? Lieutenant Price is going to be a very popular character. He has a lot of great one-liners. Those are the kinds of things you hope for. That's what goes down in history. Can you imagine the eighties without cult classic movies?"

Kent laughed. "Life moves pretty fast," he began.

"If you don't stop and look around once in a while, you could miss it," Gregory finished the quote. "Ferris Bueller was a genius."

"I took a day like that after I saw the movie."

"You did?" Gregory lifted his arm as the woman working on the jacket ran her hand over the fabric.

"Yeah. Went bowling. Watched a movie. Even went to the library."

"Library? That's not the same day Ferris had."

Kent nodded. "The librarian was a friend of my mother's. She mentioned how she'd seen me that day and I got caught."

"Ah, but you lived on the wild side for one day."

"Sure."

Gregory slipped out of the jacket, and the woman hung it up on the rack before she returned with another. This one would be worn in the scenes after his spaceship crashed. It was not as nice as the first, but that was the fun in wardrobe fittings.

"Are you heading out?" Gregory asked.

"Yeah. I have a few rewrites for the battle scene that they want. I just wanted to stop by and say I think Audrey got your flowers."

Gregory tugged on the ripped jacket and smiled in the mirror. "I'll call her later. Thanks for doing that for me."

"Sure. Hey, Bethany wanted to know if you'd like to come for dinner when you're done."

Gregory turned to look at him. "At your house?"

"Yes," Kent said pushing up his glasses. "If that works for you. I suppose we could go out, but Bethany thought..."

"I'd like that," Gregory interrupted. "Thank you."

"Sure. I feel obligated to tell you that I think she's feeling you out."

"Why would she do that?"

"Audrey."

The smile came easily as Gregory tugged off the jacket and handed it to the woman to hang up. "Making sure I'm a good person?"

"I don't know for sure. She mentioned inviting Audrey too," Kent said scratching his head. "Unless you don't want her at dinner."

Gregory made sure not to let the laugh that built in his chest escape. "I would love to have dinner at your house. And it would be even better if Audrey were there."

Kent smiled. "Great. Great. I'll let Bethany know. Tomorrow at seven?"

"Seven works. They only have me on the schedule until four."

"Next week we'll have some long days ahead of us."

And that said a lot, Gregory thought, as the woman working on his wardrobe brushed her hand over his pant leg. Sixteen hour days loomed in the near future. What had he started?

Guilt swirled in his belly. He was beginning something with a woman, who was already hesitant, but their schedules were about to tear them apart before they even began. That guilt turned to depression in a swift moment, and he breathed through it. Well, what did he expect? This part of his life was routine. He should have thought about that before he kissed Audrey during their walk—which he'd scammed too.

Kent looked at his phone when it dinged. "Gotta go. Bethany's already looking for me. Married life, huh?" He tried to look depressed, but Gregory could see through it. There was absolute bliss on that man's face.

Kent raised a hand in a wave and walked out of the room.

Gregory stood in front of the mirror as the woman tugged on his pant leg. Someday maybe he'd have that same blind bliss on his face when his wife texted him—someday.

11

Gregory reclined on his bed, and Black Sabbath laid across his feet, snoring. It certainly was better having him there, he thought. And if he could make it happen, the dog would never leave his side again.

He flipped through the channels and stopped when Deadpool flashed on the screen. Dropping the remote, he humored himself with the rawness of the movie. It encompassed everything he loved about making movies. Sure, anyone who might see him filming wouldn't think it was much. The sets looked rough, and green screens were abundant. It took a lot of concentration to perform scenes when the set itself would be added later. And anyone who thought it was easy to act in a high-tech sci-fi never had to perform with a tennis ball on a stick, which, if done right, would be a ravenous alien causing havoc in the universe.

Black Sabbath lifted his head, yawned, and shifted his position. Gregory smiled. He loved that dog, mostly because he loved Gregory back.

The thought of love, even the kind he had with the big, noisy dog, made him think of the sexy hair stylist whom he hadn't seen all day. He picked up his phone and scrolled through the contacts until he came to her picture. The thumbnail photo was gorgeous. That moment in the street, her hair swept up, and the deep neckline of that fantastic dress he'd bought her, it took his breath away.

Looking at the time, he realized it was getting late. Perhaps he'd text her instead of call.

You are on my mind. -G

He picked up the remote and changed the channel as he waited for her to reply. Instead, his phone rang in his hand.

Black Sabbath lifted his head and watched as he slid his finger over the screen and placed it to his ear.

"Hello?"

"It seems as though you've been thinking of me all day," Audrey's voice soothed like satin over him.

"What makes you say that?"

"I received an amazing bouquet of roses today with the same message as your text. And imagine that I had no way to thank you—until now."

He chuckled as the dog moved closer to him and he ran a hand over the dark fur. "Now you have my phone number. Feel free to use it."

"Someone in your position shouldn't just give that number out," she warned.

"Only people I trust have it."

He heard the sigh. "You trust me?"

"Looks like it. I got a dinner invitation for tomorrow night."

"I did too. Any chance it's at the same place?" She laughed, and it zipped through him, filling his chest with warmth.

"Your sister's house?"

"Sounds like we're having dinner in the same place then."

"Let me pick you up," he offered as he rubbed Black Sabbath behind the ears.

There was a moment's silence, and he worried that he'd crossed a line somewhere, but he waited.

"Did you really have Kent call the florist and give them my address?"

He paused petting the dog. "Yes. I wanted to protect your privacy. When you give me your address, I'll know it's okay for me to have it."

"Just like you giving me your phone number?"

He chuckled again. "Yeah."

"Then I'll let you pick me up. I'll text you my address."

"Appreciated. I'll pick you up at six-thirty."

"I look forward to it," she said. "Oh, and thank you for the flowers. They are beautiful."

"So are you. And you're welcome."

"Good night, Gregory."

He felt the embrace in her words. "Good night."

A moment later his phone buzzed again, and he noticed the text message. A photo of her bouquet accompanied her address.

Gregory rested the phone on his chest and closed his eyes. Perhaps he'd sleep well tonight.

THE LARGE BOUQUET of roses on the table was a conversation starter for Audrey's clients who arrived through the morning for their appointments. Not wanting to divulge anything too personal, she let them think they were a congratulations gift for the new salon, and left it at that.

After four haircuts and a basic color touch-up, Audrey headed to the salon where Russell and Gerald were busy working on the flooring.

"You guys are making some great progress," she said as she stood at the door and looked in.

"Yeah, we're doing okay," Russell said as he sat back on his heels. "Gerald thinks you should buy us lunch."

She laughed as Gerald wiggled his eyebrows at her. "I could really use a big pizza," he offered.

"You don't say?" She checked her watch. "Sausage?"

"Only way I eat it," he agreed.

Russell shook his head. "That's boring. It needs pepperoni and some veggies too. Geeze, don't starve me."

"I'll make it work," she offered. "How far do you think you'll get today?"

Russell shrugged. "I'm going to say half because I really want to finish this up by tomorrow. Lydia has a few more things she wants to do at her house, and at some point, I need to work on my own house."

"I appreciate this," she said as she slid on her sunglasses. "You guys are the greatest."

"That's what family is for," Russell called out after her as she turned and left the store.

As she walked past the flower shop, she noticed Bethany inside. She pushed open the door and warmed at the smile her sister offered.

"Hey, your shop is coming along nicely," Bethany said.

"It pays to have a talented family. I'm headed over to get a pizza for the guys. Would you care to join us for some lunch?"

Bethany's eyes grew wide. "Oh, I'd love that. With Kent working so much on this movie, my schedule is a little wonky. I forgot to pack lunch, and I didn't even go to the store because I knew he wouldn't be around for dinner most nights."

"Except for tomorrow, right?" Audrey laughed. "You are making dinner for us since you invited us?"

Bethany laughed. "Of course." She grinned as she slid a plump rose into a bouquet. "I think it'll be an interesting night."

"Why's that?"

"A couples' night with my sister," she paused, "and her man."

Audrey stared at her and her mouth opened to protest. "He's not my man."

"I hear he's smitten with you."

"Doesn't mean I'm claiming him."

"Yet."

"Seriously. It's a phase, and you know as well as I do that when he packs up his dog and his life to head back to California, this smitten thing will be over. I'm not buying into it."

Bethany shrugged. "For one night it'll be nice." Her smile eased into a hint of sadness that clouded her face. "I guess I should have asked if it was okay with you to have you both there. I don't get to entertain too much."

"Don't get all sad on me. It's fine. I just don't want you reading into it, that's all. Sure, he's a super guy, but he's an actor, and you know that..." She stopped and swallowed back her words, but she saw the anger flash in her sister's eyes.

"Yeah, I know. They're no good for anyone."

"I didn't say that."

"You didn't have to. Maybe you should talk to Kent and see what reservations he has about it. I mean he did marry a washed-up Hollywood addict."

They'd had this misstep more than once since Bethany had moved to Georgia. And usually, it was Audrey's mouth that started it. So she walked around the counter and pulled her sister into a hug.

"I'm sorry. You know I don't think of you like that."

It took a moment, but Bethany eventually agreed. "It's different out there. But not everyone buys into it. He's different, Audrey."

She knew that. She knew it deep in her soul. But could she believe it? After all, she'd only known the guy a week.

"I'll let you know when I'm back with pizza. Call Pearl and Lydia and see if they want to come over, too."

"Why don't we eat at the reception hall? It's cleaner over there," Bethany offered, as Audrey walked to the door.

"It's a date. I'll be back in a half hour. Round the troops."

Audrey started down the street toward the Italian restaurant on the corner. It had been there as long as she could remember. It was a staple for her father for a long time. Because he didn't know how to handle the nights he had his kids, they'd go to the restaurant, order pizza, and he'd shell out quarters to each of them to play the arcade games in the back room. He had to have spent a small fortune just to keep them occupied, but they didn't care. They all four were together, and that was what mattered during those times. She and Pearl only got to see their brothers on special occasions or when the entire family would meet for dinner at their grandparents' house. Then it was them and their cousins, and Audrey adored those times as well. Sadness filled her chest when she thought that Bethany had missed all of that. She'd only ever come to Georgia a few times when she was younger. But what was important was that she was there now and they were all together. She'd do anything for her brothers and sisters, and she knew, in turn, they'd do anything for her.

Audrey opened the door to the restaurant and walked to the counter. She ordered a couple of pizzas and a salad. While she waited, she walked to the back room and looked at the video games, which looked to be the same ones from her childhood.

Would her children play there, she wondered, and then laughed to herself. She was already thirty-one. Time was slipping to think of a family of her own. Then again Eric and Susan were having a baby, and Eric was already forty. Maybe there was time. She'd always been sure not to rush into marriage and family. It spooked her. And why not? She'd yet to see a marriage work—except for her grandparents and her aunt and uncle.

When had she become so closed minded, she wondered? A few unfortunate circumstances seemed to have clouded her mind.

When they called her for her order, she gathered the pizzas and the bag with the salad and started back toward the *Bridal Mecca*. It seemed to her she needed an attitude adjustment. This Negative Nelly wasn't going to cut it if she did truly want to find some happiness in her life.

Her mind wandered to the upcoming dinner she'd be having at her sister's house. Maybe if she shared in her sister's optimism, it wouldn't be as bad as she'd already made it out to be. After all, she did like Gregory Bishop, and not just the look of him. No, she didn't think it would work out in the end, but maybe it would for the moment. Wasn't it worth giving a chance even if it only brought her happiness for a moment?

12

One more turn in the mirror and Audrey decided to change her clothes for the fifth time. She wasn't sure what she was expecting. It was only dinner at her sister's house. That had always been casual. Why was she worried about the dress code?

She spun one more time in the sundress with the cropped sweater she'd put on. It was cheery, she thought, with little rosebuds and the scooped neck. And when she heard the doorbell, she knew that it was the final choice for the evening as she had now run out of time.

As she hurried down the hallway from her bedroom, her heart kicked up its pace. Gregory Bishop was about to step into her house. Certainly, this wasn't the time to get star-struck. After all, she'd already kissed the man. Oh, and what a memory that was. That would keep her warm on cold nights.

She pulled open the door, and he stood there, a god in denim, she decided. The corner of his mouth turned up into a shockingly sexy grin. His sunglasses hooked in the front of his deep blue T-shirt which stretched nicely over his well-built physique.

He scanned a look over her. "You look fantastic," he said.

"You too. Come on in. I just need to get a few things."

Gregory stepped inside, and she caught the scent of him as he did so. Any part of her that hadn't turned to jelly just by looking at him certainly did with the scent of his cologne.

Audrey turned, shut the door, and when she turned back, he quickly pulled her to him, pushing her back against the door, and covering her mouth with his.

Her body lit in heat and an explosion of tingles that raced from her toes to her head. She wrapped her arms around his neck as he deepened the kiss which was full of power and pleasure.

Teeth scraped, tongues lashed, and breath was fought for. Would her sister notice if they were late? At that moment she wasn't sure she could stop with a kiss, not when his hands skimmed her arms and then her hips.

Gregory stepped back after a moment and swallowed a breath. "Sorry. I've been thinking of doing that all day. I should have had a bit more control."

She wanted to agree, but how could she? "It's a nice way to say hello," she said catching her breath. "Where's your dog?"

"With my assistant. I'll pick him up when we're done with dinner."

Audrey pressed a hand to her chest, where her heart still raced. "I'll get my things," she said again and this time moved past him quickly to collect her purse and her phone.

They managed to make it out to his car without touching each other, which she figured took a lot of strength on both their parts. After all, her heart still hammered in her chest. One more kiss and they'd have been naked on the floor, she was sure of it. And it would have been her making the first move because something about the man had her gears spinning. Forget that he was named the sexiest man in the world. Forget that his annual income was more than she would see in her entire life. He'd asked her to dinner, bought her a dress, sent her flowers, walked his dog with her, and then, in her own home, he had kissed her senseless.

As he pulled open the door, he moved in to take a bouquet of flowers and a bottle of wine off the seat. When he stepped back, he smiled. "You can't go to someone's house without taking something, right? My mother would be disappointed in me if I did such a thing."

She had to remind herself to close her mouth, as she knew she stood there gaping at him. "Bethany will appreciate that."

Audrey lowered herself into the seat, and Gregory handed her the flowers and the wine before he walked around the car to get in the other side.

As they drove through town, Audrey let her mind happily spin. She went to her sister's house for dinner often. But tonight, it was different. In fact, she couldn't remember ever going to dinner at one of her siblings' houses with a man. Perhaps a barbecue at Jake's with someone casually, but this, this was wine and flowers. She swallowed the lump that formed in her throat.

"Something on your mind?" he asked as he reached for her hand and locked their fingers.

She looked at the innocent gesture and sucked in another breath. "Just taking it all in."

A smile settled on his mouth as he drove. "We have some heat."

"Yeah," she sighed and then winced at how pathetic it sounded. *Heat.* Perhaps that was all it was. Even a man brought up to take flowers and wine to someone's house could be all about sex. In her head, the thought spun that he'd only be there a few months. Relationships weren't started or guaranteed when people dropped in and then moved on. But she didn't want to focus on that. She wanted to enjoy this moment with a man that women would fight over, and he was right there, holding her hand.

She was a decent and attractive woman. She had a good head on her shoulders, and she'd always made her own way. Why wasn't she deserving of a man's attention—even a famous man.

"I'll be on set for the next three days solid. Fourteen to sixteen hour days. But I thought maybe on Sunday, if you're free, we could go on a picnic or something."

"I'd like that."

He gave her hand a gentle squeeze. "Would you like to see the set and my trailer? I could take you there. The set will still be working. They're shooting scenes I'm not in that day."

The anticipation of seeing a real, working movie set excited her. "That would be fun."

"It's a date," he confirmed as he took a right at the light.

Audrey eased into her seat. Another date. Who would have thought? She was comfortable with him. And he must be comfortable with her or he wouldn't want to spend his free time with her. After all, he had a dog, a new town, and very little time off. So for him to want to spend it with her said a lot.

Maybe for once in her life she could just calm down and accept that.

When she did calm down, she realized that Gregory navigated the town as if he'd lived there for years. He'd never asked her for directions to Bethany and Kent's house, but he was driving as if he knew right where he was going.

"You've been out here before?" she asked as he turned down their street.

"Nope. Studied my map before I picked you up. Kent gave me the address."

She nodded. "You're resourceful."

"I memorize a lot of things. It comes naturally to me."

"Not me," she said with a shake of her head. "I'm lucky to remember my keys each day."

"I don't understand geometry," he offered as he pulled up in front of her sister's house. She shifted to look at him, and he laughed. "You cut hair. It's angles. If you don't understand angles and how they work, you can't cut hair, right?"

She gave it some thought. "Right."

"We all have our strengths."

So he wasn't a snob, she decided as he climbed from the car and she opened her door. How refreshing.

13

B y the time she was out of the car, he was right next to her to take her hand and escort her to the door.

As they neared the house, the door flew open, and a fresh-faced Bethany stood there with her red hair wild over her shoulders. She wore a sunny yellow dress that accented her natural coloring. Audrey had always nursed a jealous streak when it came to Bethany. Once it was because she lived in Hollywood, and Audrey hadn't known that wasn't a good thing then. Then it was the sheer beauty of her sister. But they each had their own assets, she supposed. Just as Gregory had said, they all had their own strengths.

"I'm so happy you are both here." Bethany pulled Audrey to her and enveloped her in a warm hug. Still holding tight to her sister, she laid a hand on Gregory's arm. "I know that your schedule is so tight."

"I live for these kinds of invitations. It's not often I'm invited to someone's home," he said warmly as he held out the flowers and bottle of wine. "These are for you," he said handing her the bouquet. "And this is for dessert. Well, the guy said it was a dessert wine," he explained, as he held the bottle in his hands.

"This is delightful. Thank you." Bethany smiled at Gregory, and then at Audrey. "Come in," she offered as she stepped back so that they could pass into the house. "Kent is in the kitchen."

Audrey led the way to where the smell of something had her mouth watering already. There she found Kent, an apron over his clothes, basting a roast in the oven.

"That smells fantastic," she said, as she licked her lips.

Kent's eyes went wide at the sight of both of them as if he'd suddenly become aware of the apron. Finishing his task, he set the baster aside and closed the oven door.

"About another half hour," he offered. "My mom's recipe. She's been keeping tabs on me all day as I've been preparing it. Video chat is an amazing thing, isn't it? The salad is something my sister enjoys making, so she walked me through that too. Would you both like some wine?"

A warmth filled Audrey's chest as she listened to him ramble. He was simply one of the most endearing men she'd ever met, and she was happy that her sister had found him.

Audrey moved in and kissed Kent on the cheek. "Let me pour it. You look as if you could use a glass yourself."

She noticed his cheeks flush from the kiss as he pushed up his glasses and then began pulling at the ties on the apron. Once he'd jerked it off, and hung it on a hook, he pulled down four glasses from the cupboard and set them on the island.

"I promise not to talk shop all night," Kent began, "but how do you feel about everything?" he asked Gregory as Audrey poured wine into each glass.

"I think it's running smoothly. The first few days are always the hardest. Everyone is still trying to find their footing. But I think since the crew are all big fans of your work, that helps."

Audrey watched her brother-in-law's eyes widen in awe of the statement. "Well, that's good then," Kent beamed as he took the glass Audrey handed him. "Here's to a good start," he toasted and they all tapped glasses.

Bethany moved in next to her husband and wound an arm around his waist. "Why don't we all head outside to the patio. It's such a nice evening."

As Audrey followed her sister and her husband outside, she felt Gregory's hand on the small of her back. Lifting a gaze toward him, he smiled, and it sent a bolt of electricity straight through her. Those eyes—they were magical. Already she knew she was getting in way too deep. There was nothing to gain from being smitten with him. Her heart was only going to break in the end. She supposed every quest for something selfish—such as the affection of a man—came with a price. So, she was prepared, she thought, as she sat down on the swing across from her sister, and Gregory next to her.

When he lifted his arm to drape it over her shoulders, she sucked in a breath. That price was going to be steep, she thought. But as he gave her shoulder a gentle squeeze, and she relaxed into him, she figured she'd pay it. But she seriously hoped it didn't break her.

Dinner conversation circled around Kent's next book and a film that Gregory was slated to start as soon as the current one wrapped. Audrey felt that pang of jealousy ripping through her again as he spoke of the cast he'd be working with in Hawaii. Just a bit too intimate for her, she thought. Perhaps when it was time to let go of him she'd be okay with it. How could she possibly compete with sexy actresses on Hawaiian beaches?

She must have reacted outwardly too, as Bethany rested her hand on her arm. "I have dessert in the kitchen. Help me plate it," she said as she rose, and Audrey followed her to the kitchen.

Bethany pulled a bowl of strawberries from the refrigerator and set them on the counter before reaching into the cupboard for four small plates.

"He seems like a nice man," Bethany said.

"Seems like one? You're not believing that?"

Bethany shrugged as she lifted the lid off a sponge cake and opened a drawer for a knife. "Maybe I should throw that back your way. I saw your reaction when he said he'd be in Hawaii working on a film. Things happen on locations like that."

Audrey pursed her lips. "I suppose if we were heavily involved, it would be a problem. As it is, this is just us having common ground—you and Kent."

"I won't lie. The night that word came in that he'd headed for Vegas instead of Georgia, Kent was pretty upset."

"I can't imagine him upset."

Bethany cut into the cake and placed a piece on each plate. "He gets fidgety, can't sleep, and he paces. Lord, does he pace." She took a spoon from the drawer and began to scoop out strawberries and lay them on the slices of cake. "He was sure they'd made the right choice, but then..."

"He figured he'd made a mistake."

Bethany nodded. "He has a lot riding on this film. It's bigger than the other ones."

"He's had a change of heart?"

Her sister stopped fussing with the dessert and turned to her. "I wasn't sold on it. I was pissed that someone would put that kind of stress on Kent. And then to hear that you were seeing him..."

"I don't know that I'm seeing him. I guess we're getting to know each other. Seriously, I've known him a week."

Bethany crossed her arms in front of her. "Have you kissed him?"

"Why does that matter?"

Her sister's eyes narrowed disapprovingly. "You have kissed him."

"So?"

"So that means you're seeing him, Audrey. Dresses. Dinner. Kissing. You're involved."

"It's not a real thing. He's only here 'til the movie is over. Besides, Kent seems to be fine with him. And you said he seems like a nice guy."

"And most people who first meet Dad think he's a nice guy too."

Audrey winced at that. Most people learned quickly that first impressions can be wrong, as she felt Bethany's impression of Gregory was wrong.

Bethany handed her two of the plates. She gathered forks from the drawer and smiled sweetly. "I don't want you to get hurt. I don't want Kent to get hurt either."

Anger stirred in Audrey's belly. "I'm not going to hurt him—Kent."

Bethany took a deep breath. "I'm sorry. I'm feeling a tad protective of my older sister."

"You had to throw in the older?"

Now Bethany laughed. "He seems like a nice guy," she said again.

"And I think he is." She set down the plates Bethany had handed her and touched her sister's arm. "I'll call this off if you want me to. It bothers you."

"I got angry at you yesterday for how you approached his being an actor and I know that was about my faults," she admitted.

"You know I don't think you have faults. I mean, look at what you've overcome. Crap," she cursed under her breath. "I didn't mean to hurt you by saying that."

"I know you didn't. I fight it every day. Some days I'm just a little more sensitive to it."

Looking into her sister's face, she could see that fight cloud her eyes. Audrey spent her days worried about her own life, and she often forgot that her sister had demons to fight every day. "I'm not going to let him hurt me or Kent or you. I think he's a decent guy who let his fame go to his head for a night."

Bethany nodded. "Be careful."

"I will be," she promised.

Bethany picked up two of the plates and Audrey followed her back outside with the other two.

THE DRIVE back to Audrey's was quiet. Gregory never claimed to understand women, but this was a clear sign she had a lot on her mind.

"Kent is a great cook. No matter how hard my mother tried to get me to cook, I never quite excelled at it," he said, breaking the silence that filled the air.

"He is," was her only reply as she looked out the window.

"Did I do something wrong?"

Now she turned and looked at him. "No. I'm sorry. Just have a lot on my mind I guess."

"Understood. You have lots going on right now."

She nodded, then turned her head back to the window. "She's worried about me," Audrey said softly. Almost so softly he had to take a moment to realize what she'd said.

"Bethany?"

She turned again. "Your Vegas trip gives her some reservation. My approach to you gives her some reservation. And her own life gives her some reservation. However, in her defense, she's a worry-wart."

"And protective of her family."

"Naturally."

He reached for her hand and linked their fingers. "I would

be too. I can't blame her." Gregory pulled up in front of Audrey's building and put the car in park. "I would never hurt you. Well, not on purpose. When people get involved, there is hurt. I'm not going to say it never happens."

She narrowed her eyes on his. "We're involved?"

"I think we established to feel it out when we walked the dog, right?"

She nodded. "Right."

"Then yeah, we're involved."

Audrey kept her eyes locked on his for a beat. "I guess I should invite you in, right? See where it goes from here?"

"And I'd say no." Regret stirred in his belly even as he said it. "I'd love to come in and see where it would go. And I know right where I want it to go. But I think we should wait. Besides I have to get my dog."

"Right."

Squeezing her hand, he opened his door and stepped around the car to the other side as she slid out. He pulled her to him and dipped his head to take her mouth slowly and thoroughly. Though he knew he shouldn't go inside with her, he wanted to leave her thinking about it. When she lifted her arms around his neck, and her body melted to his, he eased back.

"I'll call you tomorrow," he said. "I don't know when, but I'll call you."

She nodded slowly as if recovering from the kiss. "Okay. Sunday? We still have a date for Sunday?"

"We do."

He brushed his thumb back over her cheek and kissed her again. She turned and walked toward the door. Gregory waited until she'd gone inside and shut the door before he let out a long and ragged breath. It had been a long time since he'd liked a woman enough to turn down an invitation to follow her into her house.

Running his fingers through his hair, he walked back to the other side of the car and climbed in. As he started the engine, he decided he'd better give this little relationship he was fighting for some serious thought. It would be a shame to lose it over a missed step.

14

Thursday and Friday, Audrey stood in her kitchen, on her feet, for nearly twelve hours each day, but it bought her a Saturday off. The salon was so close to being done that if she could just get a few full days in there to help Russell and Gerald finish up, she could get open and get people out of her house.

She loved what she did, there was no question there, but she despised having people in her personal space. Of course, she was counting her blessings. Her clientele had nearly all followed her. She'd lost a few, but usually, those were the ones you didn't mind losing anyway. But the faster she could get her salon in order, the quicker she could get back to work as normal, and home could then be an oasis.

Audrey stood in the middle of the empty salon, after a full day of punch work, as Gerald called it. She leaned her chin on the broom in her hand and looked at the gleaming floor and the freshly painted walls. They had come yesterday and put the lettering on the windows. *Audrey's Salon and Boutique*. It shimmered as brightly to her as she assumed a Hollywood movie marquee would for Gregory.

Suddenly she couldn't wait for him to see it. In one week it had gone from dirt floors and bare, roughed-in walls, to a beautiful space where she would start a fresh new adventure. The inspector would come on Monday, and if everything went well, she'd be cleared to occupy the space. The very thought made her giddy.

She was still gazing at the space when she noticed the woman standing in the doorway. Straightening, she gripped the broom in one hand. "Hi. Can I help you?"

"I assume you're Audrey?" the woman asked as she looked at the lettering on the door as if to assure she got the name right.

"Yes."

"Nichole," the woman stated boldly as she walked into the space and held out her hand to shake Audrey's. "I'm a stylist. New to town. Looking for a place to start up."

"Oh, well, I..."

"I have fifteen years' experience, but let's face it, we all did this long before we were licensed," she joked, and Audrey nodded, remembering when she had first colored Pearl's blonde locks with Kool-Aid. "I just relocated to Georgia from Colorado. So, as I said, I'm new to town but ready for a fresh start."

Audrey stood just staring at the slender, tall woman in front of her. Her dark hair bounced in subtly highlighted ringlets at her chin as she looked around the space.

Audrey hadn't been thinking of hiring anyone, especially anyone new to town without a clientele, but this woman, though full of energy and an obvious optimism, gave Audrey a peaceful feeling. Her gut said to keep talking to her.

"You just moved here? So you have no clientele?" she asked, but hadn't meant for it to sound so snide.

"I've picked up a few people in the month we've been settling in. But doing hair in the kitchen is a pain in the ass."

Audrey laughed. She knew that truth too well.

Nichole continued, "I have three kids. Twin sons and a two-year-old daughter. You can't work with them underfoot. Luckily they are in a great daycare situation for the summer. And lucky again, the entire staff needed a stylist. I put in a good twenty hours at home a week. It's not enough, and I can offer you more, but it was a start."

It was impressive, too. This woman, in a short time, had established enough clientele to work from home twenty hours a week. Audrey knew stylists that had worked years and not been able to do that. "Tell me about yourself."

Nichole pulled a piece of paper from her purse and handed it to Audrey. "Here's my resume," she said as she handed it to her. "I've worked in salons since I was fifteen. Started at the front desk, went to school, apprenticed, and then managed. After ten years I moved to my own salon with two other stylists, and now I'm here. I'm trained in multiple color lines. Up-to-date on cutting techniques and I'm an expert at brow waxing. If you're offering spa services, I'm available to do those as well while I'm building. But my expertise is in cutting and color."

The resume and letter of recommendation backed up what she had just told Audrey. It was impressive, to say the least, she thought, but this wasn't in her plans.

"It looks like you're about ready to open," Nichole said looking around the space. "I'll bet you do a lot of business with the bridal store. It's a great opportunity for referral."

"It is, and we do."

"I have extensive experience with up-dos. It's all on my professional Instagram, which I've listed on my resume."

Audrey looked at the paper to see that she did, in fact, have her social media covered, professionally. She hadn't even gotten into that as much. Proof she'd become too comfortable in how things were.

At that moment the kiss she and Gregory shared as they'd

walked the dog flashed into her mind. He'd taken her out of her comfort level the moment she'd met him—and she liked it.

"I'm waiting on approval for occupancy," she told Nichole. "I don't have a solid start date."

"I have no doubt you'll be up and running soon."

"Equipment is supposed to arrive late next week."

"I'm handy with a wrench, and I have a strong back. I'm happy to help you set up."

Audrey thought for a moment longer. "I think you'd be a fantastic addition to the salon. I'd appreciate your help getting it set up, if you can manage it."

"As I said, the kids are in daycare while I work. I can manage it. But don't you want to look at my work first?" She nodded toward the papers in Audrey's hand.

"I'm going with my gut this week on some very big decisions. I like what my gut is telling me."

Nichole's face lit up with a radiant smile. "I appreciate the opportunity, and I won't let you down," she said as she shot out her hand and Audrey shook it.

"Why don't you come in on Monday and we can go over some paperwork. The inspector should be here then, and we can begin to move forward."

"I'll be here. I'll work on some social media and ad campaigns too. I mean I'll bring them so you can approve. This is going to be a great opportunity for me, thank you." She waved as she turned and walked away, or was she skipping, Audrey wondered as she watched her.

Lydia walked through the door. Her head turned as she watched Nichole climb into her car and drive away.

"Are you already turning down customers?" Lydia asked as she walked into the space.

"I just hired her."

A crease formed between Lydia's brows. "Why? Don't you think you should get open first?"

Audrey nodded. "It just felt right. I can't explain it."

"You don't have to. I get it. I just hope you made the right decision."

"Me too," she said as she laughed.

"I'm headed for a supply run and thought I'd see if you needed anything to stock up here. Soda? Snacks? Paper towel?"

"I have a list in my bag." She walked to the back room to where she'd set her bag on a folding chair. Pulling out her list, she looked it over. "Are you sure you..." She trailed off as she watched Lydia looking out the window with intent. "What's wrong?"

"There was some guy outside with a camera. He had it pointed at your space, and then he walked right over and took a picture through the window. When I made a move, he took off."

"What?" She hurried to the window to look for herself.

"He's gone."

"Why would someone do that? A spy or something?"

"Maybe it has to do with that girl you just hired."

She shook her head. "No. I don't think so." She stretched her neck to get a better look down the street. "Maybe it was the sign people just getting a photo of their work."

"Maybe," Lydia said as she eased back. "Do you have your list?"

Audrey handed it to her. "You're sure?"

"I have the truck, and I'm going anyway. But you'll have to help me unload." She smiled as pulled her sunglasses from atop her head and put them on before giving her short dark hair a combing with her fingers.

"I knew there was a catch."

"Big wedding next weekend, I want to get everything

stocked. They're doing the rehearsal dinner at the Garden Room."

"I heard your mom added a new gazebo to it," she said, relaying the news she'd heard from Pearl about Lydia's other venue.

"It's beautiful. You'll have to come by and see it."

"I'm sure I will. Between all the weddings that are planned in our family alone, you're going to be one busy woman."

"I'm banking on it." Lydia pulled her keys from her pocket. "I'll be back in a few hours."

As she moved to the door, Officer Phillip Smythe walked through it. He took off his hat and gave them each a nod. "Audrey. Lydia," he offered, his voice lingering on her name.

"I knew it was time to get out of here." She shifted past him. "Tell him about your stalker. It'll keep him busy," Lydia grunted as she quickened her step to walk down the street.

"One of these days she'll be happy to see me," he said smiling through the pained look on his face.

"She's playing hard to get."

"She's been doing it for years now. What's this about a stalker?"

Audrey flicked her hand through the air as if to whisk away the thought. "She said some man was taking pictures of the storefront. I figure it was the sign people taking pictures of the work on the windows."

Phillip turned his head to look. "They did a fine job."

"They did. It's more official looking," Audrey said with a voice full of pride. "I don't think it was anything."

"Heard you were seeing Gregory Bishop."

"We've been spending some time together this week. Why does that matter to you, or anyone for that matter?"

He shrugged. "I've been informed that the media is taking up space in the hotels in town. Might be someone looking for a scoop."

Audrey's shoulders dropped. "They're spying on me?"

Phillip ran his hand over the brim of his hat that he held. "Might have been the people who did the lettering on your window. Just saying I know they're looking for some stories on the movie, or they wouldn't be here, is all."

Audrey let out a long breath. "I didn't even think about that."

"Keep it in mind." He ran a hand through his hair before putting back on his hat. "Where did Lydia head out to?"

"Supply run. She was getting me a few things. She'll be back in a few hours."

A tight smile formed on his lips. "Maybe I'll happen back by in a few hours and give her a hand."

With a courteous nod, he headed back out the door, and she was sure she heard him begin to whistle.

Phillip Smythe had been sweet on Lydia for as long as Audrey could remember, but he was getting nowhere with her. What made him want to try so hard, she wondered.

Then she thought about what he'd said about the media. Surely they'd want to know what the proclaimed sexiest man in the world was doing with his time in Georgia. Well, he was spending it with her, a lonely hair stylist. Wouldn't that be worthy of a story on Entertainment Tonight?

She looked around the space that she'd put her heart, blood, sweat, and tears into. She couldn't afford for anyone to mess it up for her. This was going to be her livelihood long after Gregory Bishop and the film crew were gone—when he'd moved on to his next movie in Hawaii.

There was an ache in her heart when she thought of it. If they were looking for a story, she wasn't it. She had nothing to offer the world in the way of gossip.

Deciding it was safer to shut and lock the door, she did so.

Tomorrow when she was with Gregory, she'd let him know that this little thing they were starting needed to end. She didn't need the hassle of it. Yeah, better to end it before it went anywhere. Her salon was the first priority, and she needed to make it work for her and her new employee.

Audrey picked up the broom and went back to her task of cleaning up the construction dust. Life had to keep moving forward.

15

Black Sabbath sprawled out on the bed, his head positioned on Gregory's lap. He snored softly as Gregory comforted himself by petting the dark fur which he'd missed so much. Having the dog with him made him feel at home, even in a hotel. His lawyer was still working on the custody of the dog, but as far as he was concerned the dog never needed to leave his side again.

The bonus was, Black Sabbath seemed to like Audrey. Of course, what wasn't to like? The past three days had been agonizing. He'd been on set as early as six in the morning and dropped back to his hotel at nine at night. They'd send up the re-writes for the next day, and he'd go over those while he ate room service. During breaks during the day, he'd sent off a few texts to Audrey, but he hadn't had the chance to have a full conversation with her. Looking at the clock on the bedside, he realized it was much too late to call. It was nearing eleven-thirty. From personal experience, he knew he wouldn't have appreciated a call at that time. It would have to wait. After all, he had all day with her tomorrow. They had a date—a plan. He could wait, he decided as he turned off the TV and adjusted on the bed, forcing Black Sabbath to stir.

After the long hours he'd worked the past three days, Gregory had hoped to sleep late, but it wasn't his style. Somewhere built inside of him was an internal clock that knew seven o'clock was much too late to sleep. Then again, maybe it wasn't an internal clock as much as the companion he kept who was nudging Gregory's arm with his nose.

"I'm up. I'm up. Hold on." He swung his legs over the side of the bed and sat for a moment as Black Sabbath nudged him again.

Next time he was on location for more than a week he was going to remember to request a rental house. He should have thought about it before he had the dog brought to him. Hotels were pains in the ass when it came to animals. Sure, the convenience of room service and housekeeping was one thing, but now he had to get dressed, take the elevator, and go outside. Sadly, he was vain enough to be worried who might see him. At least he was a guy. No makeup needed. Baseball hat and he'd look like he was going out for a run.

As he slipped into a pair of running shorts and a T-shirt, he thought that since he was up anyway, maybe he'd just take a run. What would it hurt? And now that he knew where Audrey lived, it wouldn't be a horrible run. It was early enough, too, that it wouldn't be too hot.

Black Sabbath nudged his leg, letting him know he was taking much too long to get moving.

"What do you say we go see a pretty lady and maybe we can convince her to make us some coffee?"

The dog whined as Gregory reached for the leash and clipped it to the dog's collar.

"I know. You could care less right now. You just need to get outside. Let's go."

Gregory hurried out of the hotel and led the dog across the street to the grassy knoll where Black Sabbath quickly moved to the nearest tree and relieved himself.

The air was cool as the sun peeked up over the tops of the trees. Usually, Gregory didn't care if he had a day off during production or not, but today he was grateful, and that was because of a woman.

Black Sabbath wandered around the tree and poked his nose into the flowering bushes that lined the sidewalk. Gregory took a moment to take in the sights for himself. The laid-back atmosphere was infectious, though he wondered if he'd ever get used to not having a highway lull him to sleep at night.

The couple who passed him, their fancy coffee house cups in hand, both said good morning to him, as did the old man on a power walk with his cane.

He'd walked far enough across the lawn, and he saw an entrance to the walking path near the river. Surely this connected to the path he had walked with Audrey. She said she lived near the path, too.

"What d'ya say we walk until we find Audrey's?" He asked the dog, who wagged his tail and gave the leash a tug.

Gregory plugged in the cross streets to his map app as he'd remembered from when he'd taken Audrey home. It would be a good two-mile run down the path, he noted, but he was headed in the right direction.

"Okay, lead the way, sir," he said to the anxious dog who took off at a quicker pace than Gregory was willing to run. Perhaps he, too, was anxious to see the beautiful brunette who had promised him her day. They'd only made it about a half mile when Gregory stopped and glanced over his shoulder. The runner, whom he'd become aware of, stopped too, and then bent over as if he were getting his breath. He gave Gregory a slight wave, which Gregory returned with a nod before letting out a low grumble at the dog who pulled against the leash. "Parasite press," he murmured, as he began his run. The last thing he wanted was photos of him running on the path with his dog to hit newsstands. He was used to it, but it pulled at him. Private life meant private life. Yeah, yeah, yeah, you didn't grace tabloid covers and expect that no one would ever follow you, but he'd hoped he'd left all those troubles in Vegas.

As he ran, he realized how much the man panting back beyond the last turn pissed him off. Oh, and there never was just one of them. They now knew he was in town and working on the film. This is where the long days came in handy. He could hide out on the set and have his driver take him directly back to the hotel after. But when he took these little side trips, that's when people noticed him.

The thought that Audrey might be too sensible to want to put up with it all crossed his mind. He certainly wouldn't want to get involved with someone who was chased down all the time.

Gregory had chosen this life. He could have long ago walked away, but he hadn't. This was the price he paid, and it was a hefty one.

Black Sabbath pulled against the leash, and Gregory picked up his pace. If he could get off the path before the photographer came around the corner, he might just lose him.

Leading the dog up an embankment, they came out to a street and hurried away from the path. The map recalculated, and he started through the streets toward Audrey's condo.

MUSIC BLARED from the little bluetooth Bose speaker Audrey had on the kitchen counter. She tucked away a strand of hair behind her ear as she pushed the mop over the floor. Having had clients in her home for the past few months kept Audrey on her toes when it came to housekeeping. She'd hoped to get up earlier that morning so that she'd been done before Gregory picked her up for their picnic. He hadn't given her a time, but she'd have everything done early, just in case he called.

The past few days had filled her head with plenty of doubt about this thing they had going on, but she was still curious. She'd give it today and see how she felt about it.

Lifting her mop into the sink, she rinsed out the head. She cringed at the hair it had picked up. If this worked out, the salon at the *Bridal Mecca*, she'd never have to do hair in her own home again.

Wiping the back of her hand over her forehead, she then squeezed out the excess water in the mop and dropped it back to the floor just as she heard her doorbell chime over the music.

She looked up at the clock on the microwave. "Eight-thirty? Who is freaking at my door at eight-thirty on a Sunday morning?"

If it was a client, she was going to lose it. That was one downfall to people knowing where she lived. Some of them didn't have that common sense filter that would tell them she didn't work twenty-four hours a day.

There was the chance it was a sibling or even Lydia. Though she wasn't sure she wanted to see any of them at eight-thirty in the morning either.

Audrey hurried to the door, pulled in her pissed off, and opened it only to find a panting Gregory and his dog.

"Hi," she said, but was quite certain her face said something different, judging by the disappointed look on his face.

"Can we come in?"

"Are you being chased?" He flashed a quick smile, then turned to look over his shoulder. "No, actually, I think we lost them. But..."

She grabbed his arm and pulled him in. "I was kidding," she

said frantically as she slammed the door, causing the dog to let out a bark.

"Shh. Not inside," Gregory scolded Black Sabbath. "I was out for a run, thought we'd head this way to see you, and some photographer must have decided to take a run too."

"So you are being followed?"

"It's normal. That's my life," he said shaking it off, but she was sure it had pissed him off too. "Have any coffee?"

"I'll make some." She looked down at the dog. "I just mopped the floor. How about you two head out to the patio and I'll bring it out. The door is just down the hall."

He didn't move at her direction, just stared at her. She realized she looked horrible. "I was cleaning. I didn't expect to see you until..."

He moved in, rested his hand on her cheek, and lowered his mouth to hers.

Warm. Inviting. The moment sucked her in until her head spun with its delight.

"I missed you," he said softly with his lips still hovering over hers.

"You did?" She sucked in a breath. "You were busy."

"Not too busy to miss you," he said before stepping back and leading the dog out to the patio.

Audrey watched them disappear outside. She took a moment more for herself to recoup from the kiss, from the shock that someone was following him, from him missing her.

A moment later she'd collected herself enough to be useful, and she headed back to the kitchen and began to fill the coffee pot with water. Pulling down the can of Tim Horton's coffee she had on subscription from Amazon, because she enjoyed it that much, she filled the filter with the grounds and started the machine. But her mind kept going back to the fact that he was being followed.

How could he be normal about people following him all the time? Just having the one person yesterday taking pictures, and she never did see them, had her locking up tight. She supposed it was something he was used to. Perhaps even Bethany was used to it. Audrey didn't like it, and she had to remember that it came with the territory if she was going to continue this—whatever it was.

Looking out the small window of her kitchen, she could see the man and the dog on her patio. It was a beautiful sight. Gregory had sat down in one of the chairs, and the dog's tail wagged eagerly as Gregory rubbed his hands over the dog's head and neck. They were their own little family, she noted. A man and his dog. It was something special.

GREGORY LOOKED up when he heard the door open. Audrey managed through the doorway with two cups of coffee and a bowl of water.

"I figured he could use a drink too," she offered as she inched the bowl toward him and he took it from her.

"He appreciates that," Gregory said as he set it to the side and Black Sabbath went directly for it.

Audrey handed him his coffee, then sat down in the chair next to him with the other cupped between her hands. "Why didn't you just call him Ozzy?" she asked as she lifted her cup to those rosy lips that kept his mind more occupied than he'd have liked to admit.

He had to think a moment about the question. "Oh, the dog," he realized, and she nodded. "The tribute to Ozzy was bad enough. Black Sabbath pissed her off more. When you know a breakup is coming, I think you automatically get vindictive, don't you agree?"

She sipped her coffee, obviously carefully considering. "I've never had a relationship like that. If you love someone or have loved someone, why would you want to hurt them in any way?" she asked as she kicked her pink painted toes up on the small table in front of them. "I don't mean that to sound as if I'm above anyone, but I've seen too much deception and revenge in my life to think that any of it is necessary."

And knowing that now only drew him closer to her, he thought. He'd seen too much deception and revenge as well, but hadn't it had the opposite effect on him? He'd accepted that and molded to it. He liked her thoughts on it better.

"How long have you lived here?" he asked looking out at the view which was a sprawling hillside that looked out over the path at the river with the city peeking up behind the tree line.

"A few years. A client of mine was selling about the time I was looking. It was fate."

"Sorta like me showing up at your salon that night, and you just happened to be there."

It should have hurt the way she laughed, but there was a gleam in her eye as she did so. That seemed to pull the pain away.

"Fate?" she choked out the word. "Oh, coincidence maybe."

"Call it what you want. I'm going with fate."

Her lips pursed now. "Fate is a big word that leads people to think there's more than there is."

"I'm up for that," he offered, keeping his eyes locked on her face, so that when she looked at him, which she finally did, she'd understand he was serious.

She worried her lip, then lifted her cup to it as if to hide her nervous fidget, which he'd found endearing.

Audrey had fallen silent, and he figured he'd pushed too far. They'd known each other a week, and though where he came from, that was sometimes cause for marriage. He knew in his heart that wasn't the way with her. She had a tainted view on relationships, though, from the few moments he was around her family, he wasn't sure why.

Black Sabbath nudged up against his leg. Gregory gave his head a rub. "Are you still on for the picnic and tour?"

Thankfully she nodded as she lowered her coffee cup. "I hadn't expected to see you this early. I was cleaning the house. I still have to get showered and do my hair."

Gregory smiled as he reached a hand to her hair which fell from its bun atop her hair. "I think you look perfect."

"Though I appreciate that..."

"I know. I'll come back by for you around noon. Does that work?"

Finally, she smiled, and it lit a fire in his chest to see it reach her eyes. "What can I bring?"

"I have it all covered. How about you bring a blanket for the picnic."

"I can do that."

With that as his cue, he stood, bent to kiss her gently, then called for the dog who obediently followed him out the door.

16

Usually picking out something to wear for something as casual as a picnic wasn't a problem for Audrey. Today, however, it was crucial. This was no yoga pant kind of day. Gregory was taking her to the movie set. A Kent Black book was a big deal enough, but this was a Kent Black movie, and big names had been called in for it. She had no idea who else she might meet that afternoon.

Her heart raced a bit faster, and she found that her palms were damp. It was silly to get worked up about it. After all, Kent Black was her brother-in-law. Bethany Waterbury was her sister, and Gregory Bishop was her boyfriend.

And that last thought had her rapid heartbeat skip and then ache. Was that what she really thought? Did she think of him as her boyfriend after a week? Now that was plain silly. She'd been the one to be so careful about it, but now the thought was planted in her head.

No. He was still just an acquaintance, who kissed like a god and looked like one too. The smile that quickly formed on her lips didn't surprise her at all. Audrey was a woman who enjoyed being kissed. There was no shame in that. It helped to remember that deep down inside he was a farm boy. They were more alike when she thought of him that way.

Audrey ran the wand of her lipgloss over her lips just as the doorbell rang. Recapping the tube, she tucked it into the pocket of her jeans, tugged at her high ponytail, and headed toward the door.

She assumed there just wasn't going to be a moment when the man didn't make her body turn to mush. Standing before her in a pair of Levi's, scuffed boots, and a basic T-shirt, he was mesmerizing.

Gregory lifted his sunglasses off his face and tucked them into the front of his shirt as he scanned a look over her. "You look gorgeous."

Audrey looked down at her white cropped pants and daisy yellow shirt which rode off her shoulders. It had been specifically put together to radiate spring and to perhaps stir him up a bit.

"This old thing?" She filled her voice with a sexy air, bit down on her lip, and batted her eyes.

She caught the hitch in his breath as he put his sunglasses back on.

"I have our picnic in the car. You choose the spot."

With a nod, she grabbed her bag and a picnic blanket off the chair and followed him out the door, locking it behind her. She stopped when she noticed the old pickup truck parked on the street and Black Sabbath in the back seat, his head poking out the window.

"Where did you get that?"

He laughed as he took her hand and walked her down the path to the truck. "I met a guy on my run back to the hotel this morning who was selling it."

"This morning? You met a guy?"

He nodded and rubbed Black Sabbath's head. "Two-hundred-thousand miles and a new set of tires."

"1984?"

"You know your Fords."

"I know this truck."

His eyes widened, and the smile remained. "Do you?"

"This is one of my cousin Eric's trucks from the ranch." She walked to the back and inspected the bumper. "This is where I backed it into a fence post when he was teaching me to drive."

"He mentioned that."

Audrey bunched her hands on her hips and studied him. That grin should have had her warm inside, but it didn't. "When did you meet Eric? Why did you buy this?"

He moved to her and took her hands in his. "I met Eric when I bought the truck this morning." Sucking in a breath, he gave her hands a squeeze. "Let's backup. On my way back to the hotel this morning I ran into Lydia. Black Sabbath loves her by the way."

"She's an animal person."

He nodded in agreement. "Somehow we got to talking about rental cars and pets. Then pickups on farms. She said that Eric had a truck over at your brother's garage that he was looking to sell cheap."

"So you bought it."

"She drove me out there to meet Eric and your brother."

Now she felt a squeezing in her chest. "You met my brother and my cousin?"

"I met them all at the ball. But yes, now I know them personally."

Audrey looked up at the dog who happily balanced his paws on the door. "He looks satisfied with your purchase."

"I think so. He liked your brother's racecar too. And his fiancée."

"I think he has good taste."

"What's not to like about a woman who is on a crawler under a car?" he offered with some humor. "When Black Sabbath climbed under with her she didn't even so much as curse. I don't think she's rattled by much."

Audrey wasn't too sure about that. Missy and Jake had spent years running each other into walls on the race track. She figured they rattled each other just fine.

Audrey moved to Black Sabbath and gave his ears a rub. Maybe she should get a dog, she thought briefly. Nah, where would she keep him? And, when the salon opened, when would she be home? But it sure would be nice to have someone to go home to each night.

The thought made her a little sad. Every day she was surrounded by people, and for the most part, when they left her, they were much happier than when they'd arrived. But still, she went home alone each night. Now with most of her siblings married, they didn't just drop by as often as they once had. Todd did from time to time if he was in town, but he lived on the ranch. It was just too far to always come into town just to ease her feelings.

"Everything okay?" Gregory's voice broke her thought as he rubbed a hand down her arm.

"Yeah. Sorry, I was just thinking." She turned to face him. "Will the picnic keep for about an hour?"

He shrugged. "I have it in a cooler in the back. Did you want to wait?"

Audrey shook her head. "No. I just thought of the perfect spot, but it's about an hour away."

The smile that formed on his sexy mouth turned her insides to mush. "More time to be with you. I'm game." He pulled open the creaky door to the truck, and she climbed inside. After shutting the door, and giving it an extra bump with his hip, Gregory skirted the front of the truck and climbed in on the other side. "Which way do I go?"

"Head northwest out of town."

17

Whenthought of Georgia, this was what he had in mind, he thought, as they started down a dirt road that tossed them around in the old pickup.

"Do I need to ask where you're taking me?" He slid her a look and caught the smile form on her lips.

"Might as well see if the truck remembers how to get home, right?"

"I wondered." He reached for her hand and laced their fingers together. "Is this where you grew up?"

The smile faded, and she shook her head. "No. I wasn't lucky enough to live out here. I always lived in town with my mother and Pearl. My cousins all lived out here on the family ranch. We each will get a piece of it to build a home on when we're ready. That was in my grandfather's plans. Todd, my brother, he lives out here though."

"He works the ranch?"

"Yeah. He's not much of a city boy. Jake is nearly all city, except he is building out here. I guess that gives him balance."

"Do you plan to build on your part of the ranch?"

She shrugged. "I've never really given it much consideration. I've always lived in town and worked in town. Don't get me wrong, the country has its charm, but..."

"It's not for you?"

She turned to study him, and he focused on the road ahead. "My father nearly lost the ranch in a poker game. Did I ever tell you that?"

"I don't think so."

"It's hard to want a piece of something that your father nearly lost for everyone. And I'm not just talking about his children. My uncle and his sons work that land. It's their livelihood. My grandfather worked that land from youth until he died as well. Then there is my father, who thinks nothing about making it a deal in a game." Her grip on his hand tightened, but he was sure she hadn't known she'd done it.

"Do your cousins or your uncle hold that against you, personally?"

The grip loosened. "No. They never have and they never will. You will not find a more gracious group of men anywhere. They gave my little part of the family so much faith in humanity when we didn't think it still existed. I'm proud to be a Walker," she said, easing back against the seat. "It's just hard to admit, sometimes, that I come from the Byron Walker side of the family and not the Everett Walker side."

"However, both sides meet up under your grandfather?"

She turned and fixed her eyes on him, and he offered her a glance. "You're right. I really should remember that when I get like this. When the road forks, take a left," she pointed toward the road.

Gregory drove until the road forked and continued. It was then the large estate came into view, and it would put a Hollywood Hills home to shame, he thought.

"That's the main house?"

"Yeah. It was my grandfather's house. Now my aunt and uncle live there and a few of my cousins."

"Where does your brother live?"

"He's in the furthest southwest corner. You can't even see the big house from his space. He has a little one-room cabin that used to house the help, years and years ago. He's happy there."

"Am I stopping at the house?"

"No, pass it and go up over the hill. You'll see another house, a newer house. We're going to go past it and toward the barn another mile down the road."

"Who lives in the new house?"

"My cousin Eric and his wife, Susan. They're expecting their first child soon. The house sits where his old house sat. It burnt down," she said, but the way her words trailed off, he assumed there was more to that story. He'd have to ask someday, but for now, he was going to drive until she told him to stop.

There was no missing the barn when he came up over the hill. It stood as majestically as the house had miles back. "Impressive."

"Eric runs all the horses with his brothers Ben and Gerald."

He chuckled. "I don't know how you keep it all straight in your head."

"It's normal to me. Pull up over there," she said pointing.

Gregory parked where she'd noted and they both climbed out. Audrey shut the door and headed straight for the barn as he opened the back door and reined Black Sabbath into his side.

Eric stepped out from inside, a cloth held between his hands. "Hey, thought you'd be earlier," he said as he moved in so that Audrey could kiss his cheek.

"I told you. I didn't know the plans."

Eric looked up at Gregory with a nod. "I'd shake your hand, but I have oil all over my hands. Tack needs cleaning." He shrugged.

"Understood."

"How's the truck holding up."

Gregory laughed. "Hasn't given me any problems in hours."

"It won't ever give you any." He shifted his attention back to Audrey. "You're all set up."

She turned to Gregory. "How big is that cooler you packed lunch in?"

"Not too big. Why?"

The smile that turned up the corners of her mouth lit a fire in his gut. "Eric saddled up a few horses for us. We can either eat later or take it with us."

"It'll travel. I'll go get it," he offered as he and Black Sabbath headed back to the truck.

Well, wasn't she full of surprises? He hadn't saddled up a horse in about a year. And as soon as the movie wrapped up, and before he headed to Hawaii, he'd make his way back to Nebraska and help his father as he did every year.

As he lowered the tailgate and pulled out the cooler, he wondered if perhaps this ride was a test. Did she not believe he was a farm boy? He chuckled to himself as he shut the tailgate and carried the cooler back to her. Why would she question that at all, he thought. Then again, he was used to people questioning his motives and picking apart everything he said. It was part of the makeup that was the business he was in. Everyone mixed up the truth and lies after a while. It was easy to do.

But as he looked at her walking toward him now with the reins to the two beautiful horses which followed behind her, he knew the feelings surging through him when he looked at her were the most truthful feelings he'd had in years. No one believed in love at first sight anymore. If you brought it up, you were crazy, but there was something here with her, he thought. What would it take for her to understand it too?

"Okay, farm boy. Show me what you got," she said, handing him the reins. "This is Fairy Godmother," she offered.

"Fairy Godmother?"

"She will give Black Sabbath a run for the best name in town."

He deserved that. "And who are you riding?"

"Mr. Melancholy."

He snorted out a laugh. "They're not race horses."

"Brothers find it humorous to one-up each other in any game."

"I suppose." He looked up at Fairy Godmother. "Will she be okay with me and the cooler?"

"She's a hefty horse, and it looks like Black Sabbath likes her."

Black Sabbath paced in front of her, and she lifted her nose in what Gregory would consider a laugh if he could read a horse's mind.

A few minutes later, he'd managed to secure the cooler to the back of the saddle and they'd each mounted. Audrey rode ahead of him, and he appreciated the view. She might have grown up in town, but she knew her horses.

Once they made their way off the road and into a pasture, she took Mr. Melancholy into a trot. Gregory hoped that Fairy Godmother could keep up, and equally hoped that Audrey wasn't going to go out into a full gallop. He did have to think about his safety when filming a movie. Nothing pissed off a Hollywood producer more than losing the head talent in a film during production. Even a trip to Vegas was forgivable.

She rode until they'd come to a fence line, then she kept with it for another ten minutes before she slowed and turned her horse toward him in front of a small grove of overgrown trees.

"An oasis in the middle of the field, huh?" he asked as the dog ran between them.

"An escape of sorts." She turned her head and looked at the trees. "Can you see the treehouse?"

Gregory looked, searching the branches. He was about to declare defeat when he noticed what might have been a sad plank in the limbs. He pointed. "That?"

She laughed, and it melted his heart. "Todd and Ben built it when they were about ten or so. I climbed up there once and fell out of the trees."

"What did you break?"

She only shrugged. "My pride. They laughed until they nearly fell out of the tree too."

"You seriously fell from that height and didn't get hurt?"

"Maybe I have superpowers."

He did not doubt that. She certainly had some power over him.

She climbed down from her horse, and he followed. "Will this work for a picnic site?"

"Better than any other I could imagine," he agreed. He lifted the cooler off the horse, and she took the reins, letting them graze just beyond the trees. Gregory took the opportunity to set up his picnic.

"You had all of this in that cooler?" she asked as she moved toward him.

Uncorking a bottle of wine, he looked at the blanket. The fruit and cheese plate, wrapped sandwiches, and a container of vegetables with ranch looked mediocre to him. Was she teasing him? Or was she impressed?

"I couldn't fit the fine china though."

She laughed easily as she lowered to the blanket and took a carrot. "My dad's idea of a picnic was buying a bucket of chicken and sitting on the tailgate of a truck."

"It has its merits."

"I like this. It suits me just fine."

He took a red plastic cup from the cooler and poured wine into it, and she laughed again. The shadows that fell across her from the tree and the hint of sunlight that played in her hair fascinated his senses. Perhaps a simple picnic did suit her just fine, but she wasn't simple. That much he knew in a week.

Audrey Walker was a force for the world to reckon with. She didn't let people walk over her, and she forged her own path. There were grudges, that was crystal clear. And, he figured, thanks to her father, she didn't trust men too well. Frankly, he was lucky she was with him in that pasture having lunch at all. Audrey Walker was fiercely loyal to her family too, and hadn't he met her when he'd gone to apologize for having screwed one of her family members over?

He handed her the wine, and she thanked him. He began to pour his own. Most days Gregory was happy with himself. Usually, he was a stand-up kind of guy, but now thinking about the few things Audrey had told him about her father, he wondered if he was a good fit for her at all.

The trip to Vegas was supposed to have been fun. Blow off the world and do what you want to do, that had been his mind-set. At the moment, it had been just that. Just as it had been crazy romantic and sexy when he'd shown up on his ex's photo shoot and carried her away, right from under the photographer and took her to Belize, where they remained naked and intoxicated for a week. That stunt had cost him a million dollars, and until that minute, it had been worth it. It had cost his ex her job as the spokesmodel for that particular perfume company. Then what did he do? He went and stole the name of the dog from her.

"Gregory?"

Audrey's voice broke the veil of shame he was hiding behind, and he realized he'd nearly filled his glass to the rim. There was no way he'd be drinking that much wine.

She reached up for his hand. "Are you alright?"

A bead of sweat rolled down his neck. "I'm fine. Got lost in thought for a moment." Carefully, he sipped the wine so it wouldn't spill out. Then he lowered himself to the blanket. Tucking the bottle into the cooler, he turned and gazed into the eyes of a woman he was only beginning to know. At that moment he realized too, he didn't like who he was before he met her. The clarity in that was shocking, to say the least.

Crazy ideas and mindless escapades seemed to be his norm, and gazing into her eyes, he'd nearly asked her to marry him— the thought had planted itself in his head and in his heart that quickly. But when she lowered her cup and set it on the ground so she could reach her hand to his face, he knew that would be the wrong move. That would have Audrey back up on that horse and heading out in a moment.

"Are you sure you're okay? You're pale."

Pushing a smile to his lips, he let the actor come through, and he assured her with his eyes that he was just fine. When she retracted, he knew he'd done a good acting job, but inside his stomach twisted. Gregory Bishop didn't want to be the selfish playboy anymore. She made him want to be better man. And hadn't he started that journey when he'd gone to apologize to Kent for blowing off their first day?

The sounds around him enveloped him. The calm and the peaceful sway of the trees and the grass in the field. Each horse made a different sound, and it was music to his ears. This was where he'd come from—simplicity just like this. The man that raised him worked harder than any studio exec, and yet Gregory didn't give him credit. Sure, he'd show up in his fancy boots and help each year, it was worth telling everyone that, too, but he didn't appreciate the man and what he did.

He sipped his wine and let it ease his mind.

One step at a time, he thought to himself, as Audrey took a strawberry and bit down on it with her sexy mouth. Right now he wanted to appreciate the glory that was in front of him, and if he could keep himself in check, maybe she'd stay a part of his life, and he'd become a better man.

side from the numerous trucks and trailers parked outside the warehouse, Audrey thought it looked average and industrial. Perhaps that was normal. After all, sets were big, right? They'd need a lot of space to build and house such a thing. But when Gregory pulled into the parking lot of the very plain warehouse, snuggled in between a produce company and a paper company, Audrey was less than impressed.

"So, this is where you go each day?" she asked as she looked around the truck trailers lined against one fence and the RVs and fifth wheels lined against the other.

"This is it."

"If I didn't know better, I'd assume you were all selling or building recreational vehicles."

He handed the man at the gate a badge, and the man looked at it, and then at him. Didn't they know who he was?

"Who do you have with you?" The man asked.

"Audrey Walker. She's a guest of mine." He turned to her. "Do you have your ID?"

Audrey nodded and produced it from her purse. Gregory

took it and handed it to the man, who then proceeded to write her name in a log. "Thank you. Good to see you, Mr. Bishop."

"Thanks, Sam."

Gregory took her ID and handed it back to her as he drove through the gate which had opened for him.

"He doesn't just know who you are?"

Gregory chuckled. "I'd be disappointed if he didn't do his job thoroughly. I have found two very admiring fans and three paparazzi in my dressing room in the past. And it was all because the guy at the gate didn't stop every car. I'm fine to hand over my ID if I have to."

"But he called you by name, and you called him by name."

"Sam does his job right, and well. My father would be disappointed if I didn't take the time to learn his name."

Audrey sat back in her seat and thought on that for a moment. She wondered if her father knew the name of his banker, his coffee barista, or his dry cleaner? It intrigued her.

Gregory drove the old pickup around to a parking lot where another man waved him through, and he parked in a designated space.

"Once you're in they don't check IDs anymore?"

"Each day a new adventure. You never know."

Gregory parked the truck, and they both climbed out. He opened the back door, and Black Sabbath jumped down, but then stayed right at Gregory's heel. This wasn't out of the ordinary for him either.

She noticed that as they walked toward the side of the lot with the trailers, he left some space between them. Understandable, she supposed. He didn't need anyone talking about him hooking up with a local. It soured her mood a bit to think of it.

"This is her," he said as they came upon a fifth-wheel that towered next to them.

Black Sabbath let out a yip as if he were backing up Gregory's statement.

"I have to assume that's the size of my condo. Or maybe even bigger."

He flipped through the keys in his hand. "I'm happy with it. Customized inside, just the way I like it."

And didn't that tell her she was in a whole different world at the moment?

"C'mon, let me show you."

Gregory started for the door, Black Sabbath right in tow.

When he unlocked and opened the door, the first thing she noticed was the scent. It smelled like him. She was truly in his space now, and it overwhelmed her.

The dog moved by both of them and bounded up the steps.

"He's happy to be home I guess," Gregory joked as he climbed the steps and then waited just inside the door for her to do the same.

Audrey took a cleansing breath and stepped up into the trailer.

She was right. It had to be bigger than her condo.

Inside he had a dark leather couch and matching chairs. A small table with chairs, not the bench seat or booth she'd seen in other campers. There was a full-sized kitchen, complete with island.

The dog ran past her as he scoped out the area. "He's happy."

"He likes it better than hotel rooms. Honestly, so do I."

"Why not stay here then?"

He shrugged. "Security. C'mon, I'll show you the rest," he said taking her hand and leading her to the back.

The beating of her heart picked up when she realized the bedroom was only a few feet away. It shouldn't have mattered. There had been absolutely no reason to assume this was why he'd taken her there. She'd found that since their kiss that morning, there had been little contact. Honestly, she wasn't sure if that was good or bad. The whole thing mixed up her head.

"Bathroom is full sized, and the bedroom has a king-sized bed," he said as he walked her through.

"And another huge TV. Why do you need so many of them? And if you don't sleep here, why the bed?"

"Some days I'm on set eighteen hours. You'd be surprised how little shooting gets done in that time. Sometimes it's a full day of them rearranging the set. Especially when you're working with special effects. They have to adjust a lot for that."

"And you work with that most the time?"

He nodded. "Especially on a film like this. Kent doesn't write things in modern day Georgia. His worlds have to be created."

"I've read the book."

"Then you know what I'm going through every day," he said with a grin as he brushed a loose strand of hair behind her ear. "Let's go on set."

Disappointment that he hadn't even tried to kiss her in the solitude of the trailer stirred in her.

She followed him back outside and waited while he locked the door. Taking the leash he had dangling from his back pocket, he clipped it on to Black Sabbath, who let out a small whine.

"You're taking him inside?" she asked.

"He'll be fine. The minute Sherri sees him he turns to mush and so does she."

Sherri Post was the woman he talked so nonchalantly about. But the raised hairs on Audrey's arms said she was a bit star-struck by the name. In a few minutes, she was about to meet someone equally famous as Gregory, yet she didn't seem to be as star-struck by him anymore. Maybe that's what happened when a man kissed her like Gregory kissed her, or gently held her hand, just as he was doing now. It was a big step, she supposed.

He was touching her in public around his people. Now the nerves were different, and her mind spun when she realized someone would see them together, someone other than the average person walking down the street.

When the security guard at the door saw them walking toward him, he stood and opened the door.

"Mr. Bishop," he said.

"Hey, John. How's it going today?"

"Doing well. Grandson lost that tooth."

"Dental floss and the doorknob?" Gregory asked with a smile.

"Wouldn't you know it, it fell out while he was talking. Tooth Fairy treated him good too." He reached down and patted Black Sabbath, then looked up at Audrey. "Have a guest?"

"Audrey Walker," he told John, who jotted her name in a log and handed her a lanyard with a visitor pass on it.

"I assume you'll be sticking with him?" He looked at their linked hands, and Audrey nodded. "Then that'll work. Have a good day."

Gregory flashed another brilliant smile at the guard and walked through the door with her.

At first, the warehouse looked like any other warehouse she might have been in. There were pallets of things, forklifts, and people moving about. But the further in they walked, the more the atmosphere changed.

Dark curtains hung from the rafters, keeping the light and the sound from entering where they were setting up a scene.

As Gregory guided them through the maze of curtains and movable walls, she saw the huge green screen where the actors were working. She'd been so mesmerized that she hadn't even seen Kent walk up to her until he nudged her.

"I'm kinda surprised to see you here," he whispered.

Once she realized who it was that was talking to her, she

enveloped him in a huge hug. "This is freaking exciting. This is your world being brought to life."

The smile that crossed his lips was infectious. "It never gets old," he whispered back and then leaned in closer. "This is getting serious, huh?" He nodded slightly toward Gregory, who was still holding tightly to her hand and the leash for Black Sabbath.

"I don't know," she said honestly.

"Be careful," was all he said before someone called him away.

That was being said a bit too often for comfort, she thought. Part of her didn't want to heed the warning. She simply couldn't imagine that there was anything to be careful about. Gregory had been nothing but a gentleman. Maybe the warning was general. But it still tugged at her.

They watched as the crew moved items around the set and the cast that was filming repositioned and went through the motions before they rolled the camera. It was fascinating to see the costumed actors interact with others who were in green suits that would then become creatures when it was all edited together. It would be easy to get sucked into standing there all day to watch what was happening, and now she couldn't wait for the movie to come out so she could see it.

When they'd called cut, Gregory walked around the cameras and crew, each of them giving him a nod or a hello. It was then she saw the voluptuous and beautiful Sherri Post. She was in full costume or perhaps lack thereof. She figured the rendition was much like that of the bikini-clad Princess Leia, which had men swooning for the past forty-some years.

People moved to her, touched up her makeup, fussed with her costume, showed her script pages, held her out a snack. Audrey was feeling a bit claustrophobic just watching how they hovered. But then Sherri saw Gregory and moved to him swiftly.

"Hel-lo, handsome," she said enthusiastically, and Audrey's insides twisted into a knot. But when the woman knelt down to Black Sabbath's level, the knot untied. "God, you're one handsome pup. I sure love that you came to visit." She rubbed his head and then kissed him before standing up. "Hey, Greg. Can't stay away?"

He chuckled, seemingly immune to her charm. "I wanted to show Audrey the set."

"Oh, the woman of the hour," she said, scanning a look over Audrey. "He told me all about you. You're opening a salon?"

"Yes. We should be open in a few weeks."

"Wonderful. Will you have pedicures? I'm going to need one once they finish putting this gold crap all over my skin." She fanned her hands down her body to emphasize the gold body paint that adorned her hands and feet.

Audrey swallowed the lump of terror that had formed in her throat. "Yes. Of course, we will have them. I don't have a card to give you but..."

Sherri rested a hand on Gregory's shoulder. "He can keep me in the loop. Kent is your brother-in-law, right?"

"Yes." The simple word squeaked out.

"He's a genius. Although I think he's watched Star Wars too many times," she said, indicating her outfit again. "Genius." She emphasized again before she was called away.

"You told her about me?" Audrey leaned in toward Gregory and whispered.

"You've occupied a lot of my thoughts this week. Is there a problem with that?"

She shook her head slowly. No problem at all, she thought. She just couldn't imagine why.

19

Gregory introduced Audrey to everyone that approached them. He'd handed off the leash to her. Black Sabbath walked dutifully between them. He'd never done that with any other woman, Gregory thought. It wasn't unusual for him to wrap himself around their legs and try to make them fall. He liked Audrey, and so did Gregory.

"Lieutenant Price." He heard the sultry voice call to him by reference to his character's name. Both he and Audrey turned to see the intern, her clipboard to her chest, her hair piled messily atop her head, and her glasses sliding down her nose. "I thought you had the day off. Did you stop by just to see me?"

Black Sabbath moved in front of Audrey, his ears pointed up, and he watched the exchange. Yeah, Gregory didn't like her either. Sensing the dog's resentment of the intern, he reached for Audrey's hand and squeezed it.

"We're just visiting," he said.

"You must be Audrey Walker," the intern said as she stuck out a hand and Audrey shook it. "Salon owner."

He saw the twitch in Audrey's brow. "Yes."

"Pepper Dawson," the intern said, and Gregory was glad she

had. He couldn't have come up with her name to save his soul. But he noticed she wasn't letting go of Audrey. "Scoping out the talent, huh?"

She ran her gaze the length of Gregory's body, bit down on her lip, then released Audrey's hand. A casual look was given in Black Sabbath's direction, but Gregory figured that Pepper wasn't dumb enough to try this charm thing on him. It was evident the dog didn't like her.

Pepper looked at her clipboard. "You're not on the schedule until tomorrow."

"Just showing Audrey around. So, I think we'll continue our tour."

Pepper nodded as she pushed up her glasses. "Of course." She gave a curt nod to Audrey and the dog, then reached a hand out to Gregory and stroked it down his chest. "I'll see you tomorrow, bright and early."

With a small wave, Pepper disappeared behind one of the huge curtains.

Gregory took in a deep breath and let it out slowly before shifting his look to Audrey, who of course stood there with eyes wide.

"Wardrobe is this way," he said as he raised her hand to his lips and pressed a kiss to her knuckles.

Audrey nodded but didn't say a word as they walked toward the room set up with costumes.

Luckily, that seemed to have piqued her interest, because the worrisome look disappeared, and wonder lit in her eyes when she saw the hundreds of costumes hanging in the room.

"Wow," was all she said, and Gregory chuckled.

"Impressive, huh?"

"I can't sew a hem straight. To think someone designed and made all of these is the impressive part."

"Hey, Greg," Priscilla said as she hoisted a battle-torn suit over her arm. "I don't have you for a fitting today, do I?" she asked as she pulled her phone from her pocket and scanned through it.

"No. Just showing Audrey the set," he offered, and Priscilla turned to Audrey as if she hadn't even seen her standing there.

"Oh, hi." From beneath the outfit on her arm, she extended a hand to Audrey. "Priscilla. Costume design. Fixer of popped seams."

Audrey's smile widened. "Audrey. Doer of hair," she joked, and Priscilla laughed.

"You're doing hair on set?"

Audrey's eyes widened again. "No, no. I'm opening a salon in town."

"Nice." Priscilla's phone buzzed in her hand. "Feel free to show her around. I have to get this on set. It was nice to meet you."

They watched as Priscilla hurried out of the room.

"Want to see what I'm wearing tomorrow?" Gregory asked as he pulled her toward a rack with multiple similar suits on it.

He pulled one off the rack that was ripped and bloodstained. There was a tag on the hanger that had the date and scene written on it.

Audrey moved her hand to touch the garment but quickly pulled back as if afraid of it. "I forgot that Lieutenant Price gets shot and dies."

"He comes back. Technology and alien know-how." He grinned.

"That's not until the last half of the book. You just started shooting."

"Not everything is shot in order. So I die tomorrow and come back to life on Tuesday in a fresh suit before our ship crashes."

Now she reached out and touched the suit. "That blood looks real."

"It's supposed to. You're supposed to want to cry when I die."

Audrey retracted her hand and clasped it with the other in front of her. "I cried when I read the book." She lifted her eyes to meet his. "Now I'm not sure I can watch the movie. That might be a bit devastating to watch you die."

Gregory reached for her hand and pulled her to him. "How about you attend the premiere with me. Then you can watch me die while holding my hand."

"You want me to be your date?"

He nodded as he raised his hand to her cheek. "I do. Have you ever walked a red carpet?"

"No."

"You'll love it. Besides, your sister will be there. It'll be a family event."

"That's a long time from now. You'll be immersed in that movie in Hawaii by the time this one is ready to release. You might not want me around by then. What if you meet someone in Hawaii?"

The room seemed to grow cold with her comment, and the pain of her words hit him right in the heart. Why wouldn't it be expected that she would say that? If Audrey wanted to pull names out of a hat, she could run him over the coals for all the brief affairs and relationships he'd had with women over the years. Usually, they were tied to a movie.

Right there in wardrobe, he pulled her to him, his hand tangled in her hair. Moving his mouth to hers, he kissed her, deeply and completely. She hesitated for a moment, then wrapped her arms around his neck as he drew her in tighter.

He didn't want it any other way. In all those past relationships, he didn't think about tomorrow—and sometimes tomorrow never came. But with Audrey, it was different. He didn't even want to think of her going to bed without him that night, but at the moment he couldn't count on that either.

"Oh, I'm so sorry," the voice came from behind them and had Audrey pulling back from Gregory.

Pepper moved toward him, a piece of paper in her hand. "Robert heard you were on set and wanted to see you." She turned toward Audrey. "He's the director," she said, snidely, before turning back to Gregory and resting a hand on his arm. "You might want to go to him alone. He's in one of his moods and all."

Pepper turned and left them alone in the room.

"I'll call a cab," Audrey pulled her phone from her pocket, and Gregory covered it with his hand.

"No. It's not as bad as she makes it seem. Let me get you and Black Sabbath set up in my trailer. I'll go talk to Robert, and then we'll get out of here."

He saw the hesitation in her eyes, but she agreed.

As they walked back out to the lot, he wondered if it had been a mistake to bring her to the set. He'd been so excited to have her see it, but he hadn't figured on her running into people.

"There's food and drinks in the fridge. The TVs are fully functioning. If the dog needs let out, there's a grass pad on the other side of the trailer for him." He pulled her to him, just as he had in the wardrobe room and kissed her. "I'll be just a few minutes. I promise. Don't go anywhere."

She promised to be there when he got back, but he wasn't so sure she would be.

20

It had been nearly an hour since Gregory had left her in the trailer.

Audrey had managed to find the remote and work the TV. She'd helped herself to a bottle of water, and Black Sabbath had led her to the grass patch out behind the trailer.

Without touching anything, she'd walked through the trailer, happy to note that the only personal effects were pictures of Gregory and his dog and one of his family. There was no doubt that the people in the photo were his mother, father, sister, and brother. It did make her mind wander to the ex-girl-friend that hadn't gotten to name the dog what she'd wanted to. Was that a thing with Gregory—always getting his way? That was a trait her father had, and it wasn't one she particularly admired.

Audrey sat down on the sofa, and Black Sabbath jumped up next to her, resting his head in her lap.

"If I didn't know better, I'd think you were doing your part to keep me cooped up in here. You knew I was thinking about leaving, didn't you?"

"I certainly was worried about it," Gregory's voice came from the door as he stepped into the trailer. "I'm glad to see he kept you here."

"That took a long time," she said as she rubbed the dog's head.

"Yeah, well, it looks like my showing up was a bad idea. They need me for a retake before they change out the set." He pulled his keys out of his pocket. "Why don't you take the truck back to your place. I'll stop by later and pick it up."

Black Sabbath jumped up from his position on the sofa and hurried to the door.

"I think he wants to go with you," Gregory insisted as he took her hand and pulled her to her feet. "Would you mind?"

Audrey took the keys he offered and looked at the dog, whose tail wagged with anticipation. "Are you sure he should go with me?"

Gregory pulled her in and pressed his mouth to her neck. Her knees went weak as the sensation of his lips on her skin traveled throughout her body. She lifted her arms to his neck.

"Yes, I'm sure," he mumbled into her hair. "I'll try not to be too late. And this way, I'm positive you'll open the door for me then and not pretend you're not home."

Audrey eased back and pressed her forehead to his. "I don't understand why you want to be with me," she admitted and hated herself for it. "I'm not the right person for you."

"Not your call," he combatted, and then took her mouth in a kiss that sealed the deal that she'd be there when he came. "Go home. I'll be along in a few hours." He brushed a strand of hair back from her face and lingered his thumb on her cheek. "I'll bring dinner."

"I'll make dinner," she countered. "Bring an overnight bag with you."

She moved out from his embrace and took the leash from its

hook by the door. When she turned back to him, he watched her in stunned silence.

"You can do that, can't you? Or is there a policy that you have to check into your hotel by a certain time?"

Gregory shook his head. "No. I can come and go as I like. I'll bring a bag. Are you sure?"

No, she wasn't sure, but for some reason, she thought it was the only way to truly know what was going on between them. She might change her mind in the next few hours, especially since she had decided to go home and Google the hell out of his name. A part of her wanted to find nothing, and make something of this crazy adventure she was on. Another part wanted to learn that he was a troll and it would be easier to cut him loose. She just wasn't sure which possibility she wanted to win.

Audrey clipped the dog's leash to his collar, and they started for the old pickup, which she was familiar with. Never in her wildest dreams did she think she'd be driving it away from a movie set with some movie star's dog next to her. But it seemed natural enough.

Black Sabbath climbed into the cab when she opened the door. She climbed in after him and started the old beast. Looking back at the trailer she watched as Gregory locked the door and started toward the warehouse, just as a hurried Pepper headed toward his trailer. Audrey slowed the truck and watched in the review mirror as he evasively moved around the woman and walked into the building.

There was something about Pepper Dawson she didn't like. A bubble of fear crept up into her chest. Perhaps she didn't want to search him on Google too much. What if the name Pepper Dawson showed up? Something told her she'd be devastated.

As SHE PULLED up to her building, Audrey noticed her sisters' cars were parked out front, but neither Pearl nor Bethany seemed to be around. This spoke intervention.

Just as she suspected, as she entered her condo, with the dog, her sisters both walked out of the kitchen. They each held a glass of wine in one hand, and Bethany held out another to her.

"And why are you both in my house?" she asked as she took the leash from the dog and reached for the offered glass of wine.

Bethany sipped from her glass. "My husband said you could probably use some company."

Pearl adjusted her bracelets, which dangled from her wrist. "He said you got stood up for the rest of your date."

"And that's all?"

Bethany shrugged. "Should there be more?" She looked at the dog that had sat alert at Audrey's feet. "Is he your guard dog now?"

Audrey rubbed his head, and he flattened to his belly and quickly fell asleep. "He's taken a liking to me."

Pearl turned and walked toward the back door. "Let's sit on the balcony."

Audrey toed off her shoes before following her sisters out to the balcony. They each took a seat, and Audrey kicked her feet up onto the table as Bethany tucked hers up under her.

"Why did Kent send you over here?" she asked, aiming her question toward Bethany.

"He's working stupidly long hours, and he's trying to keep me busy," she said.

"I love you, but I don't think you're telling me the truth."

Bethany studied her for a moment. "He's worried about you. When people get involved in a movie, and they're secluded with those people in an intimate situation, things happen. Relationships build and tear down quickly. He just doesn't want you to get your heart broken. You have a lot going on."

Audrey sipped her wine. "I'm a grown woman. I can handle myself."

Audrey figured it was true. She was a grown woman who could take care of herself. After all, she'd been doing it for years.

Her father had never been much help, except to cause more problems in town. It never was a blessing to be Byron Walker's daughter. And of course, her mother, while that was an entirely different story, she was needy. Oh, so needy.

Pearl was always more diplomatic than Audrey was. Audrey flew by the seat of her pants, perhaps that is why she was opening her salon. Had she not flown off the handle when she found out about the sale of the salon where she'd worked, and had planned buy, she might still work there.

But then, where was the adventure in being calm, and pleasant? Audrey was on an adventure. She thought of it as Walkers' spirit. Walkers did what they wanted to do, and tried not to get in anybody else's way. Except for her father.

HER SISTERS HAD STAYED PERHAPS an hour. It had been a nice visit, but she'd rather have been alone. With the dog at her heels, all she could think about was the moment that Gregory arrived.

Would she tell him that she saw Pepper Dawson go to his trailer? Admittedly, he looked to be avoiding her. But there was something about the woman, she thought. The way she talked to him. The way she looked at him. The way she had touched him.

Hadn't she been telling herself all week not to worry about it? He was going to Hawaii to film another movie. He was leaving. That needed to be the end of it. She didn't want it to be. She wanted to feel out this new adventure. Even if it was for only a few more weeks.

At peace with her decision, she rubbed the dog's head as

they walked through the house to the living room and both reclined on the couch.

When the doorbell rang, Audrey sat up, and Black Sabbath let out a large bark. She hadn't realized that she'd fallen asleep. And the dog must have too.

He accompanied her to the door, and she flicked the lock without even a thought. But then, she thought about the person who had been taking pictures outside of her salon. And then she thought about the impromptu run Gregory and Black Sabbath had taken earlier that morning. Inching up on her toes, she looked out the peephole on the door and was grateful to see Gregory standing there.

A smile slid over his lips as she opened the door. He looked tired. Perhaps he wouldn't stay after all. But then she noticed the bag that sat on the ground next to his feet.

"It looks like you had a rough afternoon," she said.

He scanned a look over her, and then down at the dog. "And it looks like the two of you took it easy."

Audrey ran a hand down the dog's back. "We had some visitors, some wine, and yes we took a little nap."

"Are you going to let me in? Or have you had too many visitors?"

She hadn't even realized she hadn't invited him into her home. And wasn't it odd that the dog stayed at her side?

Audrey stepped back, and Gregory picked up his bag and walked through the door.

There wasn't another moment like there had been earlier. She hadn't been pushed up against the door. There was no romantic interlude. There seemed to be something on his mind.

"Can I offer you something to drink? I have some wine. I also have a few beers in the refrigerator if you're interested."

The smile that formed on his lips was weary. "I'll take one of those beers."

"Make yourself at home on the couch. I'll get the beer."

He did as she said, and the dog followed him this time. Perhaps the dog understood that there was something wrong.

As she walked to the refrigerator and pulled out a beer, she thought about Gregory's mood. She'd seen it before. Her sister Bethany, too, had been as worried, or so it seemed. Was this the same kind of thing?

In her mind, putting a movie together wasn't that big of a deal. Wasn't it all feeding egos? Sure, there were long hours, but honestly, how could there be any stress?

She turned to the drawer next to her and took out the bottle opener. She pulled the top from the beer and discarded it in the trash. Replacing the opener, she shut the drawer with her hip and took a moment to collect herself.

It was called justification, she thought, this maddening thing going through her head. Every person that she knew had told her to be careful. Now, there sat a moody man in her living room, and she didn't know him well at all. But he was there. And she asked him to bring his overnight bag.

She looked at the beer in her hand and wondered if she should offer it to him. Her sister, at her lowest, had been addicted to prescription medication. Nobody had known at the time. But the look on Gregory's face was too familiar to her now. Would this beer send him over the edge?

The dog walked into the kitchen and straight over to her. She wondered if she would miss Gregory as much as she would miss this damn dog when he left. Black Sabbath seemed to nudge her out of the kitchen and back toward the living room. Gregory sat on her couch, his head tipped back, his eyes closed. The gentle sound of his breath told her he had fallen asleep.

It gave her a moment to study the man, without him knowing. Did a man, as famous as him, fall asleep in just any woman's house? Was his comfort level so great with her that he could simply fall asleep?

She set the beer on the coffee table in front of her. Taking the TV remote, she muted the sound. That seemed to wake him up.

He sat up and rubbed his eyes. "Sorry. I guess I fell asleep."

"It's been a long day. It's nearly ten-thirty."

"I have to be on set at six in the morning." He moved his head from side to side as if to stretch out the kinks in his neck. "Is this beer for me?" He asked nodding toward the beer on the table.

"Yes."

Gregory picked up the beer and took a pull from it. He let out a refreshed sigh. "Thanks. I needed that." Looking up at her he said, "can I convince you to share it with me and sit here on the couch?"

He didn't look as depressed now as he looked tired, she thought. She damned her cynical mind for always making the worst of something.

Audrey sat down right next to Gregory, took the beer from his hand, and took a long pull herself. Black Sabbath hopped up next to Gregory and laid his head on his lap.

"Goofy dog thinks we're at home. I'm sorry he's jumped up on your furniture."

She looked at the dog so comfortable on his owner's lap. "We were napping together on the couch earlier. He's fine to stay there."

"You're a very accommodating hostess," Gregory said. "I should probably take him back to the hotel. Monday morning's going to be here awfully early." He reached his hand up to her hair and gave it a stroke. "I guess you have to go to work tomorrow too."

"I don't usually work on Mondays," Audrey said. "I'll go in

later in the morning and get some last minute details put together on the salon. If everything goes right, I can open the doors next week. I won't have a grand opening for a few more weeks. But anything to not work out of my kitchen anymore."

He brushed the backs of his fingers over her cheek. "I'm proud of you for what you're building," he said.

It struck her as odd that he would be proud. "How can you be proud of somebody you don't know."

"I know you better than you think I do. Why can't I be proud of you?"

"I guess in my head, and you can only be proud of somebody if you've known them their whole life."

He brushed his fingers down her throat and over her shoulders. "Well, now you know you were wrong." He grinned at her.

The feelings that were taking over inside of her were conflicting with one another. He was a stranger. He was a gorgeous man. She hadn't known him but a week. Certainly wasn't long enough to feel the things she was feeling. Every person she knew had already warned her to be careful. So why, as she looked into those deep blue eyes, did she feel the pull to keep him near?

Audrey licked her lips, as her mouth had gone dry. "Do you have to go back to the hotel?"

His fingers had moved back to the side of her neck and gently feathered intimate touches on her skin.

"I don't have to go back at all."

"Stay here with me. Spend the night with me, in my bed."

There was a flash in his eyes she hadn't seen before. He no longer looked tired. He no longer looked depressed, or upset. Perhaps her eyes matched. Because in his eyes, she saw desire.

21

Gregory managed to maneuver himself out from under the sleeping dog. He took Audrey's hand and pulled her to him.

"He'll be asleep for hours." His hand wandered down her back. "But we'll wanna leave the bedroom door open for him. Sooner or later, he's going to wonder where he is. And in turn, he's going to come looking for us."

"Not a problem," she said breathlessly as his hands wandered over her bottom and back up.

Gregory pressed a kiss to her lips, and she swallowed the panic that had begun to bubble up inside of her. Sex wasn't a new thing to her. Sex with a stranger wasn't even a new thing to her. Why did this feel so different? Something tugged at her heart. Something she'd never felt before.

Gregory's lips slipped from hers and moved down her neck to that delicate place on her collarbone that made her moan without even thinking about it. His hands moved under the hem of her shirt and pressed against her skin. Warmth. Electricity. It all mixed and made her dizzy.

Audrey pulled from him, taking his hand. "I can't stand here much longer. My knees are going weak."

The smile that crossed his lips now was nearly devious. "I could carry you, if you'd like."

The offer let that bubble of panic slip through in the form of a choked giggle. "I'll walk, but I think we'd better hurry."

She tugged him down the hallway, afraid to look back, afraid to lose her nerve. The moment they stepped over the threshold to her bedroom, he spun her around and lifted her off the ground. Her arms instinctively wrapped around his neck, and her legs did the same around his waist.

Gregory's fingers were knotted in her hair, and his mouth had found hers. The kiss was hotter than any that had come before it. The warmth of it, in anticipation of it, and its execution had her clinging on as if it were for dear life.

Gregory walked across the room until his knees hit the bed and he dropped them both down onto the mattress. "I'd have liked to have taken this a lot slower," he said as he tugged off his shirt. "Remember that I'm promising you one slower."

She heard his promise but simply didn't see the need for it. She was as rushed as he was. Pulling off her shirt, she saw his gaze linger. Appreciation? Dear God, she hoped so.

When she released the front clasp of her bra, his mouth opened.

"And when we go slower," he said as he slipped off his pants. "I'm going to leave the light on and enjoy every single moment."

SLEEP DIDN'T COME AS EASILY as Gregory had hoped. Exhausted, was an understatement. But how could he sleep when the woman he was falling in love with was wrapped in his arms.

He hadn't meant to fall in love with her, he knew. It wasn't the way the game was played. New town. New woman. No regrets. But this was so much different.

Sex had been incredible. He'd had enough sex to know that this was outstanding. He had lingered in a woman's bedroom with them wrapped in his arms before. So why did this one feel so right? Perhaps it was the dog laying across the end of the bed over their feet. Even with his ex, the dog never did that.

He anticipated the alarm on his telephone to go off any moment alerting him that it was time to return to the studio. He loved his job. Nothing would ever change that. But what he wouldn't give for a few days to never leave her bedroom.

When the dog's ears perked up and sent him sitting up on his hind legs, Gregory took note. A moment later he heard the crash as if somebody had knocked over all the pottery on the balcony.

The noise was enough to wake Audrey up from her deep sleep. She came up so fast that their heads collided and her scream had Black Sabbath yelping a loud, disturbing bark.

She quickly covered her forehead with her hand, and he saw the tears welling in her eyes. "Are you okay?"

Audrey winced but nodded. "I'm fine, but what the hell was that noise?"

"Something outside," he said as he tossed his legs over the side of the bed and pulled on his pants. "You stay here," he told her. "We'll go find out what happened."

He snapped his fingers, and the dog jumped off the bed and moved right in beside him. God, he loved that dog.

With his phone in his hand, he used the light as a flashlight to guide him down the hall. It was times like this that he wished he was as brave as the characters he played in movies. But the truth was, this scared the hell out of him.

It wouldn't be the first time he'd had someone stalk him, but he didn't want anything bad to happen to Audrey. She didn't deserve that.

The door to the balcony was still closed and locked, but from the window, he could see that the furniture had been toppled. Perhaps someone was trying to get in and fell over the small table.

"What is it?" Audrey whispered from down the hall.

"The table got knocked over."

"Is the wind blowing?"

He wondered if she'd buy it if he told her it was, but he decided against that. Nothing good ever started out with a lie. "No. I think someone was here and kicked it over when they ran off."

"Someone was here? At my house?" The volume of her voice rose with the panic. "Oh, God."

He and Black Sabbath moved back to her. He took her hands in his—they shook. "You're safe."

"How can I be safe if I have people up on my balcony? It's not like they just wandered through my yard."

"Let's get you packed up, and you're going back to the hotel with me. There's security there. Tomorrow you'll call the police."

She nodded. "I'll let Phillip know," she said as she turned back to her room.

He didn't know who Phillip was, but she seemed calmer by wanting to discuss it with him.

Within a half hour, they were driving away from her building and headed toward the hotel. Time was quickly slipping from getting any good sleep before he had to be on set. This was one of those days he dreaded, fourteen hours of work when his mind was already mush. If he ever were hired for another movie after this one, he'd be surprised. Then again, there were working actors who were far worse than him at being exhausted and unreliable.

22

They managed a few hours of sleep, and Gregory figured that was good enough. He had breakfast sent up to his room, and while Audrey was in the shower, he took Black Sabbath outside for a quick walk.

While outside, he called his manager and told him about what had happened. He told him about the person following him on the path the other day. And he complained about Pepper Dawson being on set. He'd been prepared for his manager to scold him for not using the bodyguards that the production company provided. Gregory still didn't think it was quite necessary. He did, however, worry about Audrey's safety.

When he returned to the hotel room, Audrey sat on the bed in a white terry towel robe, the TV news on.

"I just realized it's six-thirty. Weren't you supposed to be on set at six?"

"I called in a few favors," he said as he unhooked the dog's leash. That was part of the phone call to his manager, he thought. He didn't know why they extended any favors to him at all after his Vegas stunt. But they had. "They are sending a driver for me. They'll be here in fifteen minutes."

"I should get dressed then. I'll be ready to go and get out of here."

Black Sabbath wandered the room as if to get a feel for the mood. Gregory sat next to her on the bed. "Why don't you stay here today. You'd be safer here."

"Don't pull that bullshit hero stuff on me," she said through gritted teeth. "I have never needed a man to take care of me, and I never will need a man to take care of me."

He let the harsh words settle, understanding that they were fueled by fear. "I can arrange a car for you. Or you're welcome to take the truck."

She worried her bottom lip for a moment. "I'll take the truck. People are used to seeing that very truck outside whatever establishment I'm at."

"And don't forget, you promised to call the police."

"I've already sent Phillip a text. He'll be at my salon around seven o'clock this morning."

"Good. I'm going to be occupied for the next few days, and I don't want anything to happen to you."

"I'll be just fine," she snapped as she stood up and went back to the bathroom, shutting the door behind her.

Gregory sat for another moment. After last night, he hadn't expected her to be upset with him. And he couldn't quite decide if she was upset with him or the situation. Either way, it wasn't looking good for him. When she emerged from the bathroom, she was dressed, and her hair was pulled back in a ponytail.

"Let me take the dog with me," she offered. "At least if he's with me today, he'll have a little freedom."

It was a generous offer, he thought. Although he was sure it had nothing to do with being generous. He was beginning to understand her, and this was her way of keeping the dog close to her for safety.

"I'm sure he'd like that a hell of a lot better than wandering around the set with other people."

"Of course he would," she bit out the words. "He'll be fine with me the entire time. No need to rush to find him after you're done tonight. I'm sure it will be late."

Gregory stood and wiped his palms on his thighs. "Okay, then let's talk about tonight. I'd be happier if you didn't go back to your house."

"And I'm not afraid of my own house. Whatever happened last night isn't going to happen again. Besides, I'll have him with me," she said as she nodded toward the dog.

"Then expect me late tonight. I'll call you before I show up," he said as his phone buzzed in his pocket. He pulled it out and looked at the display. "My ride is here. I need to get going."

Audrey quickly gathered her few items that she had brought. Then, she grabbed the leash and hooked it to the dog's collar. "Is there anything I should know? He's not some special Hollywood dog, is he? Does he need certain kinds of food? Seltzer water? Perhaps I should book him for a doggy massage," she snapped.

If she were any other woman, he would've walked out of that room with the dog and never looked back. It wasn't like that with this one. He'd let her have her moment. She deserved to be a little bit angry.

"He's your normal average dog. I know he'll be fine with you." A few moments later they were in the lobby and going their separate ways. He had given her the keys to the pickup truck that once belonged to her family. And he climbed into the black sedan that would take him to the set.

As the car pulled away from the hotel, he turned around to watch her walk the dog to the pickup truck and let him inside. His stomach knotted, and his heart rate quickened. The thought that somebody could hurt her made him sick. Was it all because of him? He didn't know her all that well. But he didn't imagine she was any kind of troublemaker.

When he had a little bit of a break, he would do some researching of his own. Not that he didn't trust her. But perhaps it would be better if he got to know her, from an outside perspective. He was used to people telling him tales to get his attention. She hadn't told him anything. But then again he hadn't asked. So who was Audrey Walker? All he knew was he was beginning to fall in love with her.

AUDREY PARKED THE BIG, beat-up red pickup truck right in front of the door to her salon. She wanted to be able to see it. It was only seven o'clock in the morning, but she didn't want to go home. No, she was going to lock herself into the salon and finish everything up. It was time to get back to work. It was time to get back to normal.

By seven-thirty, there was a knock at the door. Black Sabbath let out a roaring bark, which had her spinning quickly around, only to see Phillip standing at the door in his uniform.

She hushed the dog and gave him a gentle pat. But he followed right on her heels as she walked to the door and opened it.

"Got yourself a new dog?" Phillip asked, as he took off his hat and made eye contact with the dog.

"He's Gregory's dog." She took hold of Black Sabbath's collar loosely, just to keep a hand on him. "Black Sabbath, this is Officer Smythe."

Phillip waited another moment before putting his hand out for the dog to give it a sniff. And then he petted him. "Nice dog."

"He seems to like me just fine."

"Can I come in, sit and talk with you?"

"Of course," Audrey said as she stepped back and let him

pass before she locked the door again. "I have coffee in the back room. Would you like some?"

"I'd like that a lot," Phillip said with a nod, and he followed her to the back of the store, with the dog still at her heels.

Audrey poured each of them a cup as Phillip sat down at the small table. Black Sabbath wandered to him, and Phillip rubbed his head. "I miss my dog. I thought of getting another. I'm just not home enough."

"This is the first chance I've ever had to be around a dog. You know how it was, we didn't have one at home."

She set a mug of coffee in front of him, and then sat across from him with a mug of her own.

There was silence between them, the kind that only old friends could have. But then he leaned in. "Tell me what happened last night."

Audrey thought about the turn of events. How much did she want to tell him? Did he already know?

"Gregory and Black Sabbath stayed the night," she said, but she heard the hitch in her voice when she did so. "And I don't want a lecture about it. I'm a grown woman."

Phillip sat back in his chair and crossed his knee over the other. "Of all people, I'm not going to be the one to give you a lecture on it. Leave that to your sisters and Lydia."

"They don't know about it yet. So I would appreciate if you didn't say anything."

A smile formed on his lips. "Might be just the kind of thing to tell Lydia to get her to talk to me." Audrey bore a stare into him, but he only laughed. "Now, Audrey, you know I'm only fooling."

Phillip uncrossed his long legs and leaned back in over the table, folding his hand around his coffee mug. "So you and Gregory and the dog were at your house. About one or two o'clock, you heard a noise as if somebody was trying to get into your house, correct?"

"Yes. It woke us up. And of course the dog..."

"One the most useful reasons to have a dog."

She'd have to agree. Perhaps if Black Sabbath and his owner ever left her, she'd have to consider getting herself a dog. "Honestly, I think perhaps the dog scared whoever it was away."

"So this sound you heard, was it breaking glass, somebody ramming the door, what was it?"

"The patio furniture had been turned upside down, Phillip. It was as if someone tried to run over it. Or use it to break the window." Though that had been the first time she considered that, and it scared the hell out of her.

"You didn't think to call the police last night?"

"There wasn't any real damage. Just a chair and a table over. And we left. I should get some credit for getting out of there."

He let out a hum and then took out his cell phone. He typed some notes in and then tucked it back into his pocket.

"I'm going to drive by your house. Why don't you give me a key and let me go in and look around."

"I don't think it's a big deal," she said, as she rose and walked over to her purse to get her keys.

"Or did you forget Lydia saw somebody take pictures of your salon?"

Audrey held the keys tightly in her hand. Perhaps there was a correlation. She turned around and gave Phillip the keys.

"Do you think I'm in danger?"

"I arrested one of my own deputies for stalking your sister. He burned down your cousin's house and shot him. I question everything." Phillip stood and tucked her keys into his pocket. "You're involved with a very famous man, Audrey. He's got some history. Do you know that?"

"I've done a little research. He hasn't done anything bad."

"He's been a little careless with people," Phillip noted.

"I'm fine, Phillip. I'm not going to let anything happen to me."

"Now, none of us are going to let anything happen to you." He turned and walked back through the salon to the front door, and Audrey and the dog followed. "Keep this door locked," he said. "Lydia knows to be watching out for you. I'm guessing my presence here will have Pearl set off as well."

"It's awfully early for Pearl to be at work," Audrey argued as she unlocked the front door.

That smirk of a smile that would cross Phillip's lips when he was happy to tell you that you were wrong, formed. And just then Pearl hurried down the sidewalk to the front door of the salon.

"What's going on," Pearl said hurriedly.

Phillip gave a small tip of the hat toward Pearl and continued to smile. "I'll let your sister tell you what's going on. Audrey, I'll be in touch."

Pearl's wide eyes set on Audrey. "He'll be in touch why? What happened to you? What did Gregory do?"

"Why do you assume Gregory did anything?" she asked, as the dog came back to her.

Pearl acknowledged the dog and then moved her gaze back to her sister. "That was official business. Not just Phillip hanging around trying to catch sight of Lydia. What happened?"

Audrey let out a defeated sigh. "I have some coffee in the back. Come have a cup. I'll tell you what happened."

23

Pearl only sat there staring at Audrey after she had told her the story. "This is like Bethany all over again. What is it with psychopaths wanting to hurt people in the movie industry?"

"I don't think this is anything like Bethany. Fine, maybe somebody was trying to get a picture of him. He's extremely famous," she said but was sure she was saying it to herself to remind herself. "I don't think anyone will hurt me."

"You have no idea what somebody would do." Pearl held up her hand as if to examine her manicure. "Why do you have the dog?"

"There are too many people on that movie set. This is nicer don't you think?"

"Nicer for who? The dog, or you?"

"I think it's a win-win for both of us," she said as she heard tapping at the front door.

Pearl stood from her chair. "You're not open. You're not expecting customers. Who is that woman?" She asked as they both looked toward the door.

"That would be my new employee, Nichole. I wasn't expecting her." Or was she? She couldn't even remember now.

Both women and the dog moved to the door. Audrey unlocked the door and opened it to Nichole whose arms were full of supplies.

"I know this is presumptuous," Nichole said. "But I saw that you were here. And I've been driving around with the stuff in the back of my car for two weeks. I was thinking if it's okay with you, can I set up a station, or put it in storage?"

Audrey smiled. "I was going to put you in that station by the window." She pointed. "The station is ready. I'm waiting for the mats to arrive today and then will put the chairs in. So go ahead, move your stuff in."

"Thank you," she said as she looked at Pearl. "I'm Nichole. I'd shake your hand if mine weren't so full."

"I'm Pearl. Audrey's sister, and I own the bridal boutique next door."

"That's great. I sense family is strong here."

"Very strong," Pearl said as she reached for Audrey's hand and gave it a squeeze.

Nichole looked back at Audrey. "Thanks for taking a chance on me. You won't regret it, either," she said with certainty.

Audrey was sure it was going to be just fine. She'd only met this woman once, but she did like her.

As Nichole moved past them over to the station, Pearl adjusted the bracelets on her arm. "I'm here 'til 7 o'clock tonight. Don't you leave without telling me you did so. I'm going to tell Lydia what happened, and Gia too. I want everyone to be aware that somebody could be around here. But we'll all stick together. Just like we always have."

"I appreciate it, but don't think I can't take care of me."

"Who knows that better than me?" Pearl looked down at the

dog. "I'm going to send Tyson to get some dog food and a bed. I think the dog would appreciate it."

Audrey looked down at Black Sabbath. "He's already so spoiled. If you do that he'll think he's a king."

"I'll bet he already thinks that," she said scanning a look over Audrey. "Lock the door. Tell Nichole what went on. It's not fair to her to not know."

Audrey gave her a nod and let her out the door. She locked it behind her and went over to Nichole who was meticulously setting up her station.

"I'm hoping to quietly open next week, maybe Wednesday. I'm ready to get my clients out of my kitchen," she said with a chuckle.

"I understand that. I'll be ready for next Wednesday then. Are you going to do a grand opening?"

"I'm sure Lydia wouldn't let me open a new store without a grand opening. She loves to plan parties."

"Lydia, she's the one that owns the building and the reception hall at the end?"

"She owns it with my sister Pearl, and her brother Tyson, Pearl's husband."

"I was right," she said with a giggle. "Family is strong, isn't it?"

Audrey picked up the frame off the station which held a picture of Nichole's children. "It is strong. Pearl, and Bethany who works at the flower shop, and I are as close as three sisters could be. We have two brothers, Todd and Jake, and we're close to them too."

"I think that's pretty wonderful. That's what I hope for my kids. That they'll grow up together and be lifelong friends."

Audrey replaced the picture and smiled at Nichole. It was too early to get into family dynamics. Sure, she was close to her siblings now, but it wasn't always that way. The boys had their life, and she and Pearl had theirs. Then there was Bethany, poor Bethany. Perhaps the best thing that ever happened to her was her coming to Georgia. At least they all understood the necessity of family, and that probably saved Bethany's life.

"So my sister wants me to make sure I tell you about some things going on around here."

Nichole stopped what she was doing, and leaned a hip against the station. "That's quite a serious tone. What's going on?"

"I just want you to be aware. I don't think there's any danger," she said, and then filled Nichole in on the happenings.

THE LACK of sleep was wearing on Gregory. The director must've noticed too, as he sent him to his trailer to get some rest. As if he was going to be able to, Gregory thought, as he pulled out his laptop and set it on the kitchen table.

He had about thirty minutes before somebody would come for him, he unzipped the coat that read Lieutenant Price and hung it over the back of his chair. When he opened his laptop, he realized it had been a while since he'd been on it.

The screen that came up was the information page for the Bellagio Hotel in Las Vegas. He cringed. In fact, the very thought of that trip made him nauseous. He guessed perhaps it was fate. Had he not taken that stupid trip, he wouldn't have gone back to grovel to Kent, and he wouldn't have met Audrey. Audrey had been the best thing to happen to him in a very long time. Something about her made him want to be normal. He loved every aspect of his job, except the fact that his head had gotten too big, just like too many Hollywood types. Well, that was for him to change.

Gregory typed Audrey's name into the search engine and waited. The normal things came up, a set of reviews for her hairstyling services, she was listed as part of the Walker family who owned the Walker Ranch, and buried at the bottom was a news article about Bethany Waterbury having a stalker who kidnapped her, shot her cousin, and set his house on fire.

Gregory sat back and let out a breath. That had to have been horrific. That went far beyond fangirls in his dressing room.

Did the person on her porch have anything to do with the stalker of Bethany's? Or was the same story playing out again?

He closed the laptop and looked at his watch. He'd corner Kent and ask him about that. He figured it wasn't going to be too long before the entire Walker family knew what happened at her house last night. He grabbed Lieutenant Price's jacket and slipped it back on. He wasn't going to let last night's incident get between them. He wasn't going to let anyone hurt her either.

As he tucked the laptop back in the drawer, the door to his trailer opened.

"They're ready for you," Pepper Dawson's voice echoed through the trailer before she stepped in.

"I'm on my way inside." He started for the door when she closed it behind her. "Did you need something?"

"You've been avoiding me since you got to Georgia. I don't like that."

"You didn't tell me you would be on this film."

"It took some string pulling, but I managed to get a position. I thought after Las Vegas you would want me here."

"Things are different here. I need to get inside. I'm guessing you can see your way out."

He didn't want to leave her in his trailer. In fact, he wanted her as far from his personal space as he could get. The woman wasn't right in the head. That came out quickly enough once he'd spent time with her in Las Vegas. One more reason to be regretting the whole trip.

Gregory walked as fast as he could to the building. He

turned back once more to look at the trailer. However, she had yet to leave. He mentioned it to the security guard waiting at the door.

"Send someone over there, will ya? She should've followed me out."

The security guard agreed and began to call for help.

As Gregory walked to the set, he wondered if it could have been Pepper that climbed onto Audrey's balcony. He wouldn't put it past her. He'd mention it to Audrey. Not the part about Las Vegas, but about her being so unstable. Maybe Audrey could tell her friend Phillip about it. She seemed to trust him.

A few moments later, all of that was forgotten. Gregory was thrust into the cockpit of his trusty spaceship, General Logan at his side. He could immerse himself into the character easily, which was a credit to him. Too many other co-stars of Sherri Post couldn't do that.

The rest of the world was forgotten, and that was why he was an actor.

24

It had become the ritual over the past two weeks, one night at Audrey's house, the next night in the hotel. Audrey would cook dinner on the nights that Gregory slept there. Room service was called upon on the nights that she stayed at the hotel. She couldn't reason that one was better than the other. She liked having him nearby. And she certainly liked the attention the hotel staff gave them.

She and Nichole had managed to put the entire salon together so that they could begin taking appointments. And just as she had assumed, Lydia had been standing right there during her break, with a notebook, ready to plan a party. So, they began to plan a party.

By the time Lydia had left, catering had been planned with Susan, her cousin's wife, her aunt had been contacted about invitations, and Bethany had been commissioned to make flower arrangements. She wasn't sure her salon could hold the number of people Lydia wanted to invite. But then, as it was pointed out, it would be a good opportunity for people to see the reception hall. Lydia was always thinking business, Audrey mused.

Black Sabbath spent his days with her, sleeping on the bed that Tyson had brought him, and she and the dog were happy.

The car they sent for Gregory showed up every morning at six AM, and it brought him back home around ten at night. There wasn't much time for socializing. He seemed to understand the necessity for a good night sleep. She could respect that. But even with him sleeping in her bed every night, she missed him.

It seemed as if they went from being two strangers getting to know each other, to two roommates who shared a bed. She didn't mind really, but it had moved much faster than she'd anticipated.

There hadn't been anybody climbing up her balcony. Though the day after it had happened, Gregory had sent her a text and said he wanted to talk about it. Somewhere in their busy schedule, they had forgotten to have that talk.

She'd gotten used to people whispering behind her back in public places. She knew the sign of a lifted cell phone to take a picture. However, since nobody bothered her, she wasn't going to worry about it. If she was going to date one of the most famous actors around, there was going to be some publicity whether it was wanted or not.

On a night when Gregory was working even later than usual, she had sat outside her sister's house drinking wine and Bethany had told her it was all part of the job. Kent was a celebrity in his own right, though he could fly under the radar, but it took him a while to adjust when people found out that Bethany Waterbury was in Georgia and they wanted her picture. Soon the hype died down. Now, they were just a married couple going through life.

There was comfort in that. Audrey didn't want any spotlight. But if she wanted Gregory, the spotlight came with him. While she was standing at the grocery store, she saw a photo of him in Las Vegas. It squeezed at her heart, she tried to look away, but to no avail. She hated tabloids, she decided as she picked it up from its stand. Blurry pictures of the man she spent every night with, his arms wrapped around some woman, stared back at her from the dull pages. She couldn't make out the face of the woman. And what did it matter, this woman came before she did. It wasn't as if Gregory was her first lover. But it hurt all the same. She wanted to believe he'd just had that urge to gamble, as he'd said the first night. Not once had she assumed he'd gone with someone else.

The disappointment wrapped around her like a rope trying to squeeze the life out of her. When he came in that night, she'd made sure she was already in bed. He didn't try to wake her. And the next morning, she waited until he had left before she climbed out of bed.

The texts came more frequently that morning. Of course, he wanted to know if she was feeling okay. When she didn't answer, he wanted to know why she was mad at him.

It was unjustified, she decided. So why was she so petty about it?

It had also become ritual for Audrey and Black Sabbath to spend their evenings lounging on the couch watching trashy TV. Now that she didn't have to worry about her clients being in her home, Audrey certainly relaxed.

Not once had she ever watched one of those entertainment news shows. She didn't see any value in them. But just as she reached for the remote to change the channel, a flash of one of them came on.

"Gregory Bishop is on the set of his new movie, the film adaptation of Kent Black's latest book." The entertainment news lady batted her extra-long eyelashes and tossed golden locks over her shoulder. "We're following up on the story that we brought you at the beginning of the filming of this production. You might remember we mentioned that Gregory Bishop missed the first day on set due to an impromptu trip to Las Vegas. Photos are just now coming out of Gregory Bishop and a young intern from his last movie."

Audrey noticed even the dog's ears had perked up and he inched forward as if he, too, were watching this.

"The trip that nearly cost Bishop the movie is now making headlines because of the intern, who is working on the current film. It looks as though she's being replaced with a new secret woman."

Audrey let out a harsh breath just as Black Sabbath let out a large bark. Only a moment later the front door opened, the dog moved in front of her as if to protect her from the person walking in the door.

"Are you two okay?" Gregory asked as he put his keys back in his pocket.

Tears were already rising in her throat. It was stupid. None of that should matter. She remembered the way that intern, Pepper Dawson, looked at Gregory when they were at the set. Every day, he spent the entire day with this woman.

She couldn't even look at him. She didn't want to look at him. Moving in the other direction, she went to the kitchen. The dog moved to Gregory and greeted him, but Gregory pushed past and followed her to the kitchen.

"What's going on?" he asked from a safe distance.

Audrey gripped the edge of the counter, her back turned to him, the tears streaming down her face. "I don't know what all of this is to you. I don't know why you come back to me every single night. This is all a mistake."

She heard him release a breath, but he didn't take a step toward her. "My publicist called me today. I'm guessing you saw some news."

"News?" She turned around. "Genocide is news. An election is news. Some spoiled actor, who blew off his first days on set, and took some young intern to Las Vegas, that's not news. That simple stupidity," she shot back and moved past him and down to the bedroom.

"You're gonna hold my stupidity against me? If you were going to do that you wouldn't have met me for that first date."

"Well, maybe I shouldn't have."

"I thought you were little more mature than to pay attention to idle gossip. You don't want to ask me about this? You don't want to know my side? You just want to be mad?"

"It feels right."

Audrey plopped down on the bed and wiped the tears from her cheeks. Black Sabbath hovered at the door as if to make sure everyone was okay.

Gregory paced for a moment, raking his fingers through his hair, and then tucked his hands into his pockets.

"I knew I should've mentioned it. I should have told you that somebody else was involved in that trip to Las Vegas. But to be honest, the whole thing didn't seem important to me."

"They said you almost got fired. How can that not be important to you?"

Gregory moved to sit next to her on the bed. He clasped his hands in front of him and set them on his lap.

"I don't want to lose you over this."

"Are you going to sit here and tell me that you thought this would go longer than the time you'd be in Georgia? If you think I'm stupid enough to believe that..."

"I do believe it's supposed to go on longer. Audrey, I've never felt about anybody like I feel about you. None of it even matters anymore."

Audrey stood and paced the room herself. "How am I supposed to believe you? Your job is to tell lies. I think you're really good at it."

She saw the hurt on his face when she said it, but she

couldn't take it back now. It would be better if he just left, and they both moved on. And when he stood, she was sure that's what he was going to say too.

Gregory moved to her swiftly. His hands came to her wet cheeks, and his thumbs whisked away the tears. Then, he lowered his mouth to hers.

She wanted to push him away. She wanted to kick him out of her house and tell him to go as far as he could. But something kept her right there pressed against him. Something she didn't want to admit was happening.

Gregory rested his forehead against hers. "Give me an hour to tell you my side. To me, this is a relationship worth fighting for. Let me have my chance to fight for it."

Audrey closed her eyes and let her body relax. She felt as though she owed him the opportunity.

She opened her eyes. "You're done earlier than normal tonight," she said realizing she hadn't even thought to start dinner.

"I found out what they were going to publish. In my mind, it's not a big story. But somebody has something to gain. All of this would be easier to fight with you by my side. But I would understand..."

"Tell me your side first. Then I'll make up my mind."

25

I t all seems so juvenile, so stupid. Gregory opened a beer, took a long, satisfying pull, and handed it to Audrey.

She took a few moments to calm down, and he was grateful. She'd had every right to be angry. He sat down next to her on the sofa and kicked his feet up on the table right next to hers. Audrey took a pull from the beer and handed it back to him.

"I know you have a fight in you," he said as he tucked a loose strand of hair behind her ear. "But I want you to listen to me before you say anything. I want you to hear everything from me because that's the way it should be. Okay?"

Audrey nodded and brushed another tear from her cheek. He let her be worked up. After all, if some ex-boyfriend were to walk through the door, he'd be a wreck too.

"She's young. Twenty-one. It shouldn't be a big deal right? But the media is going to make it bigger. That's the job. It was a fling. Nothing more than a fling." He took another long pull from his beer and handed her the bottle. "The money gets to you. This status, the way people treat you. You absolutely forget who you are. And that's what happened to me."

"I get that," she said softly handing him back the beer. "Bethany went through all of that. So, I understand that part. I'm sure I would've been the same."

Gregory pressed his head against hers. "The story wouldn't have been anything important. If it weren't for you."

Her back had stiffened, and she sat up straighter. "Are you telling me this is my fault?"

"No, not at all. What I'm saying is, the public is used to me well, being a playboy I guess. Trust me, that's not the image I want to portray. But again, you get caught up in it. So fine, they have photos of me here and there with people, and now, if they're following me, they see that I end up at home every night with the same person. It's different."

"You keep saying that. A relationship needs to be specific. There are ground rules."

"Exactly, and that's why I don't want this to get in the way of what we have. This, this is a relationship. The two nights I stayed in Las Vegas with her was a fling. And they're going to make you out to be some secret woman. There already going to put out pictures. It'll only be a day or two before your name is associated. I don't want this to hurt you."

"Is this what you wanted to talk to me about after that first night we spent together? Do you think she was the one on the balcony?"

"I don't know. All I know is that I've asked for her to be removed from the set more than once. She seems to hold some clout."

"She's an intern. How much clout can an intern have?"

"It sounds horrible, but I suppose that would depend on who else she is sleeping with. This is how ladders are climbed." He finished the beer and set the empty bottle on the table. "My point is, I made a mistake. Even if I had never met you, it would've been a mistake. They're going to track you down. I don't want that to affect you. And I don't want it to affect us. I like what we're building."

"What can happen when this movie is over? I live here. My roots are here. My business is here. This is where I belong. And a relationship is hard enough when two people live in the same house. What are we going to do with this?"

"We're going to figure it out. Audrey," he purred her name as he turned to take her face in his hands, "I have been thinking about this. I've never felt what I feel for you with anyone else."

She shook her head. "Don't. Don't drag this out."

"It's not dragging it out. It's finalizing it." He locked eyes with her, keeping his hands right on her face. They weren't in the same mindset right now. He knew that. But he had to tell her how he felt. "I love you, Audrey." He took in a hard breath and chuckled. "Oh my God, I've never said that to anybody."

He watched as her chest rose and fell quickly with her breath. "Never?"

"Never. That's why I want to fight for this. Those pictures are about to come out. Those news channels, those stupid entertainment news channels can make you out to be something you're not. So I need you to know; don't believe any of it. When this movie is over, and I go on to filming in Hawaii, I'll take you with me if I can. But," he held up a hand to stop her interruption, "I know you have a life here. It's worth me finding out if I could have a life here too."

Audrey lifted her fingertips to her lips. "You'd stay here?"

He pulled her to him. "Pretty sure this is where my dog wants to stay."

She laughed against his chest, and he held her tighter. For a moment, just one moment, the situation had been defused. But when the pictures came out of the two of them together, and they built Audrey to be the bad guy, the secret love, it would be an uphill battle. He was sure Pepper had instigated the release of the pictures, and any story that went with it. That just made him repeat, in his head, what a mistake it had been. It would go away. Sooner or later no one was even going to care. Once that happened, they could move forward.

26

Audrey was exhausted when she unlocked the door to her salon. The night hadn't gone as she had planned. Her heart still ached, and her stomach was tied in knots. But Gregory had said those three little words that no other man had ever said to her. She deep down wanted to believe them, because she was sure she felt them for him as well.

Just as she turned the key in the lock, the figure caught her eye. She pulled the keys back as if to put them in her fingers like a weapon, and spun around quickly. Her cousin Ben jumped back from her, his hands up in surrender.

"Whoa," he said. "I was calling your name. Your head is somewhere else."

Audrey caught her breath. Her heart rammed in her chest. "What are you doing here?"

"Well, I happen to be your first client of the day. And I was going to get us some coffee first. Although I'm not sure you need any coffee."

Audrey put her hand on her heart. "I forgot you were coming. Actually, I could use a coffee. I'll go get set up, and I'll be ready when you come back."

Ben studied her for a moment more, then smiled at her. "I'll be right back."

She opened the door and watched him walk down the street. Instinct told her to lock the door behind her, but normality told her to leave it open.

Black Sabbath had gone with Gregory that morning, but now Audrey wished she had taken him with her. It was stupid how dependent she had become on that dog. He gave her a sense of security. Well, hell, maybe she should think about getting a dog.

She moved through the salon forcing herself to do things as normal. Turning on the lights, she checked the temperature and then stored her bag in the back. Audrey flicked on the music, and the speakers filled the room with some easy listening acoustic guitar.

For a moment, that was all she could take. Perhaps later they would crank up the 80's channel or something. But for now, she needed to calm.

By the time she got settled, the front door had opened again. Nichole walked through with her large bag over her shoulder and a wide grin on her face. She stopped, noted that somebody was walking toward her, and held open the door for Ben.

"The best clients are the ones that bring treats," Nichole joked as she let Ben into the salon.

Ben looked at her, and Audrey could have sworn he swallowed his tongue. "Yeah."

She held back the laugh that bubbled in her throat. Oh, wasn't that cute? Ben was smitten. It would be interesting to see if he could even have a conversation with his own cousin while Nichole was around.

"Did you have them make it extra strength?" Audrey asked as she walked toward him.

He looked at her blankly. And then down at the coffees in his hand. "Normal," he stammered as he handed her a cup.

Nichole set her bag in her chair and pulled out a few dollars. "I think I'm going to walk down there and get me a fancy cup too. That woman I had yesterday, the one who wanted her hair tipped blue and she was like eighty, she tipped me forty bucks. I figure I got coffee for a week." She smiled widely as she strolled back out of the salon.

Ben's eyes followed her. Audrey slapped him on the shoulder and brought him back to reality. "Dude, your eyes are going to roll out of your head."

"I heard you had a new employee. But, wow."

Audrey laughed at her cousin and sipped her coffee. This was exactly what she needed, a moment of family to reel her back in. From here on out, the day would only get better.

By THREE O'CLOCK in the afternoon, Audrey's shoulders hurt and her feet ached. All of that was normal when her schedule was as packed as it had been. And even when her back began to ache, she looked around her little salon and she was happy. This was exactly what she wanted. Perhaps Jake was right. Fate had stepped in the day she walked out of that other salon.

Just as she had sat down in her chair, moments after Nichole had left for the day, a man walked through the front door. Audrey stood to greet him.

"How can I help you?"

"Do you take walk-ins?"

"Of course." She'd said the words before she had thought it out. She had one more hair color to do, and then she could go home. But, money was money.

Audrey looked up at the clock that hung on the wall. "I have about a half hour before my next client. I could do you now."

"That would be fantastic. I'm on a tight schedule too."

"Great. Come on over."

Audrey went through the motions just as she would with any other client. She escorted him to the shampoo bowl, washed his hair, and gave him a scalp massage. She walked him back to her chair, and when he had sat down, she wrapped the cape around him.

"Just trim it up?"

"Yeah, thanks. So, your salon is pretty new, huh," he asked as he kept his head still and his eyes darted around.

Audrey pulled a comb from the drawer and began to comb his hair. "We've only been open a few weeks. Just getting started."

"This is a nice area. I'm just visiting really. I'm working with the movie."

Her face flashed her surprise. She had caught her expression in the mirror. "Oh, the author of the book is my brother-in-law," she explained, without going into further detail. "What do you have to do with the movie?"

The man didn't answer right away. "Photographer."

She wanted to dive in a little more. After all, what a great opportunity to have somebody that was working on the movie come right into her salon. Had Gregory sent him?

"That must be pretty fantastic," she said just as the front door to the salon opened again. Madison Jantz strolled in, her arms full of bags from the local merchants. "Hey, Madison, I'll be just a few minutes."

"Take your time," she said as she dropped her bags into a chair in the waiting area. "I just stopped by Gia's store, oh my goodness. She just got a new shipment in from Italy. I had to stop myself. I could have bought it all up."

It brought a smile to Audrey's face and to her heart to hear somebody talk that way of her cousin's fiancée. Of course, now she would have to see what Gia just got in.

Audrey finished up the haircut, and the man looked pleased enough. She escorted him to the front desk and typed the haircut into the computer.

"That'll be thirty dollars," she said looking up at the man.

He handed her a fifty. "Keep the change. I appreciate you getting me in on such short notice."

"Are you sure? It was my pleasure."

"Absolutely sure. I'll make sure to let Pepper know she was right, this was a great place to come," he said as he turned with a small wave and walked out the front door.

Audrey dropped down in the chair behind the counter. Her hands shook. And once again, her heart ramped up in her chest.

Madison walked over to her. "Are you okay? Can I get you some water or something? You're awfully pale."

Audrey sucked in a deep breath. "I'll be fine. I must've just got hot. Give me just a moment."

Madison agreed, but watched her as she stood and walked to the back room. Audrey pulled her phone from her bag and looked down at the screen. No text messages, no phone calls. She pressed a hand to her stomach, and it turned just by the thought of the woman's name. Why was she still on the set? She didn't trust the woman.

Audrey tucked the phone back into her bag and took a few deep breaths. She wondered if they'd let her on the set. She took her phone back out and texted Kent. He would be easier to reach. She asked him to leave her a pass, and she'd be there in two hours.

Luckily, he texted her back quickly. *The pass will be waiting for you.*

She tucked the phone back in her bag. Perhaps facing the problem head-on would make it go away.

27

The moment Audrey was done with Madison's hair, she headed toward the set.

As promised, Kent had a pass for her waiting at the guard station. The guard checked her in and told her where to park. He informed her after that she'd have to check-in with another guard station.

Luckily, she had been there before, or she might have been completely lost. As she made her way to the guard station, she spotted Black Sabbath being walked by a young man in the lot. The moment the dog saw her, he started for her, tugging at the leash and forcing the man to follow. Audrey knelt down and snuggled the dog.

"I'm sorry, ma'am. He's a little cooped up right now."

"He's been staying with me an awful lot. I think we have a really good relationship." She scrubbed behind his ears and then stood up. Holding out her hand, she introduced herself. "I'm Audrey Walker, a friend of Gregory Bishop's."

The man's eyes grew wide. "Oh," he said as his voice dipped. "Um," he stammered some more as he looked at Audrey's badge. "You're all checked in?"

Audrey studied the man and tried to get a feel for his strange behavior. "Yes, Kent Black is my brother-in-law. He arranged for the pass."

The man gave her another quick study. "I thought you were someone else. So, which one are you here to see? Kent or Gregory?"

She smiled coolly at him. "Whichever one is easier to find."

The man ran his hand over the back of his neck. "Well, I think that would be Gregory. Kent was busy in his office doing some rewrites I think. It's been a really busy day."

Audrey reached for the leash and took control of the dog. "Can you lead me to Gregory then?" She asked the young man.

He nodded and started for the door.

She couldn't help but wonder who he thought she might be. Maybe the woman she came to confront wasn't even there. Was it possible Gregory was able to get her thrown out? A little bit of her wished so— hoped so.

The set was noisy. People moved pieces around, and she noticed that the costume woman was adjusting Sherri Post's wardrobe. As they walked around the draped walls, she saw Gregory. He was in costume.

A strange sensation washed over her. He was dressed in a flight suit, that looked as though it had been ripped to shreds. His face was bloodied, and his hair a mess. The sight did something to her. It tore her up a bit. Yet, on the other hand, it was eerily attractive.

As if he sensed them, Gregory turned and a smile lit his face. He held up a finger to whomever he was talking to and headed directly for them.

"Dear God, you are a sight for sore eyes." He lifted his hands to her cheeks and kissed her lips hard.

Audrey noticed the reaction of the young man that stood

next to her. Gregory turned, gave the man a nod, and a moment later he disappeared.

"What are you doing here?" he asked as he rubbed the dog's head.

"I had a busy day. I just felt like coming by. I hope that wasn't a problem," she offered, hoping it didn't seem like a lie.

"Not a problem to me. Although, if you're going to stay around, you'll have to watch me die about four more times."

She chuckled. Never in her life did she think a man would say that sentence to her.

Deciding to poke for some information, she thought she should tell him about her customer today. "I had a walk-in today. A photographer. He said he was part of the movie. I forgot to get his name. He tipped me twenty dollars."

Gregory's eyes widened. "That's a lot of money for a photographer."

"I thought so too. He must've had the day off. I don't see him around."

"I can't even imagine who you're talking about." He pointed toward the set where another man was taking still shots. This man had a long ponytail that hung down his back. "He's the only photographer I know of. But, this crew is huge, I don't know everybody."

She wondered if she should even mention the name Pepper. The man said she had sent him. But, as she didn't see Pepper anywhere either, perhaps it was better just not to mention it.

Somebody on the set called Gregory by name. He acknowledged with a nod. "Are you going to stick around? Let me rephrase that. I'd like you to stick around."

"I think this could be fun. I know how the book ends. So I know that if I watch you die four times, you'll come back to life."

He brushed his thumb over her cheek and laid another kiss

on her lips. "Nothing can take me away from you, doll." He gave her a wink as he walked back toward the set.

Audrey found a corner where she could sit down, hold tight to the dog, and watch as Gregory died over and over again. The first time, her eyes welled with tears. By the sixth take, she found that she had to stifle a giggle.

After the take, the set grew noisy again. Gregory was whisked away, and Audrey sat where she had been for the last two hours. She saw Kent, being directed by the young man she met outside. He gave her a wave and started toward her.

She stood as he neared, and gave him a warm hug.

"Kent, this is amazing to watch. I thought the book was good. But watching it come to life— that's freaking cool."

He smiled so wide that she thought perhaps it touched his ears. He pushed up his glasses and then gave his hair a brush to the side with his fingertips. "It is fun, isn't it? So what are you doing here?"

She thought about her answer for a moment. This was Kent. There would be no lying to him or even dodging around the truth. He'd been one of the first to warn her to be careful. Maybe he knew all about Pepper Dawson.

"I had a walk-in today. A man, I never got his name, but he said he was a photographer on the movie."

"Good. Part of doing a production in town was to bring more revenue to the area. I'm glad everybody's using the businesses around town."

Audrey bit down on her bottom lip. "While this particular individual was there he said he'd been referred to me. Obviously, I assumed either you or Gregory would have sent him, but he said Pepper sent him."

The moment she said the woman's name, Kent's eyes flashed that panic she'd seen in them before. She hit something there.

All she could hope now was the Kent would spill the information.

"Pepper? As in the intern, Pepper Dawson?"

Audrey gave a casual shrug. "I would assume so. Why does that seem to startle you?"

He shifted his body weight as if to change his body language. "Do I look startled?"

Audrey nodded. "I know who she is, Kent. I can only assume she sent the man to spy on me. Gregory seems to think she's the one leaking these private photos and stories of them. I can tell you, I was just trying to get the bottom of it."

Kent moved in closer to her. "Gregory had her removed from the set days ago."

Gregory hadn't mentioned that, which upset Audrey. "So then she did send this guy to spy on me."

"I'm not comfortable with that. I'm going to make sure Phillip puts some detail on you."

"Right, because that won't scare away my clients."

"I'd rather have you alive than working on clients," Kent said.

Audrey found that she was gripping tighter to the leash. "You think she's that big of a threat? You think she'd try to hurt me, or us?"

"I have no doubt she was the one on your balcony that night. It's just a hunch, but if I went with my gut, that's what I think."

"But if she got kicked off the movie, wouldn't she have left town?"

Kent scratched the back of his head and then tucked his hand into his pocket. "I heard she never got on the plane. They arranged for her travel, and a car to pick her up. But she didn't go. That leads me to believe she's still in town."

Resigning to the fact that Gregory spent a weekend with a psychopath, Audrey decided perhaps Kent was right. "I'll call

Phillip. Maybe you're right, and it would be better if I had some-body with me, or if I didn't go in for a few days."

"You're surrounded by family, Audrey. No one is going to let anybody hurt you. Between your brothers, your sisters, and your cousins, everyone will be around you. But do tell Phillip. I'd feel better if he was around you too."

Kent's phone buzzed, and he pulled it from his pocket. "They need me. Gregory might be a few more hours, are you going to stick around?"

Even though she was growing bored, she didn't want to go home. "Yeah, I think I will stick around."

"I'm going to have somebody find you some food and some water. Him too," he said, nodding at the dog. "You let me know when you do leave. I want to make sure Gregory is with you."

"I will."

Kent reached for her hand and gave it a tight squeeze, then he turned and disappeared.

Audrey sat down in the chair she'd occupied for hours. Black Sabbath walked over to her and rested his head on her lap. She ran her hand along the length of his back. "You won't let anyone get to me, will you?" she asked the loyal dog. His answer was in his actions, she decided, as he raised his nose, looked at her, then circled and laid on the floor across her feet.

28

Once Gregory's overdone death had been finalized, he, Audrey, and Black Sabbath headed to the hotel. He didn't speak to Audrey the entire drive because it had been Kent who told him that her walk-in client had been sent by Pepper.

He realized, as he drove up to the hotel, he'd been clenching his jaw, he was so angry. Angry at Pepper for pulling such a stunt. Angry at Audrey, for not telling him first-hand what happened.

She'd been on the phone with Phillip Smythe most of the ride from the set. He was going to have a car drive by her place every half hour. And, because he could hear him speaking so loudly through the phone, had told her he'd be in touch with her family. Gregory assumed that meant there'd be a perimeter of Walkers as well.

As he pulled the old truck up in front of the hotel and left the keys in the ignition for the valet, he let out a long breath to defuse his anger. His presence in that town was causing a lot of problems for Audrey and her family. None of this would've happened had he not been part of this movie. But he couldn't put it all on himself. There was no way to know this would happen, or that he would have fallen in love. And he did, he did love her.

He took Audrey's hand and interlaced her fingers as they walked into the hotel. As they rode the elevator to his floor, she leaned against him in an intimate gesture that told him she trusted him.

Because he was starving, he ordered up room service. Then, he filled the bathtub with the luxurious samples they had left for him. "You're going to take a bath, and I'm going to take the dog out. Lock the door. And I will call you on my way back up."

He noticed the hesitation in her body, but she never said anything. Pulling her to him, he tipped his lips toward her ear. "They have more security. I will be fine. I know what you're thinking."

Gregory heard the deadbolt lock as he stepped into the hallway with the dog. He walked toward the elevator and pushed the button, saying hello to the security guard who was stationed there. Once inside the elevator, he placed a phone call to his mother. Once he told her what was going on and making her promise to ensure that she took care of herself, he placed a similar call to his brother and his father. He wanted everyone to be safe. He figured his sister was fine in Japan. But he would call her, too, in the morning.

IT HAD TAKEN a lot of argument, but Audrey finally convinced Gregory that she could drive to work without any problem. She had already heard from Phillip, and he had promised to be at the salon when she got there. Of course, she had Black Sabbath with her, too.

She wasn't, however, prepared to see Phillip standing in front of her salon window which had been broken in, and was shattered all over the sidewalk.

She held tight to the leash, keeping Black Sabbath from the debris. "Dear God, when did this happen?"

"Not sure. My guess is not too long ago. We didn't get a call on it yet. But it looked like this when I walked up," Phillip said adjusting his hat. "I think you're closed for business today."

"Dammit! This has gotten out of hand. I could kill her myself."

Phillip rested a hand on her shoulder. "Take it easy. Someone has to have cameras around here. It'd be a good guess that Lydia does," he said just as Lydia turned the corner and stopped short from stepping on glass.

"Holy shit!" Lydia looked at the mess on the sidewalk and then at the hole in the front of the salon. "What happened?"

Phillip took off his hat, gave Lydia a nod, then replaced his hat. "Vandalism. You got video cameras around here?"

Lydia's face grew hard as she fisted her hands on her hips. "You know damn good and well I have cameras here, Officer Smythe," she said his name with a bite. "And, you know I'll let you see them."

Audrey noticed the smile tugging at the corner of Phillip's lips, but it never did quite surface. "You have some orange parking cones?"

"You know I have those too."

"Why don't I follow you back to the reception hall. You pull up the footage. I'll get the cones. We are going to set them out here as we get this cleaned up." He turned toward Audrey. "You come with us. We'll go in the back door. Let's see if they did any more damage."

Audrey agreed with a nod, and with her hand tightly wound around the leash, she led Black Sabbath out of harm's way and toward the reception hall.

Phillip retrieved the orange cones and set them out front. Then he and Audrey walked through the back door of her salon.

"I need to call Nichole, quickly. She has clients in about an hour. I'm not supposed to start until ten."

Phillip narrowed his eyes at her. "You both will be canceling those appointments," he said with that demanding tone that she'd grown to loathe. "Nobody's working here today. You need to call your sisters and Gia and let them know what happened."

"You can't have them close their stores because of this. What if something just happened?"

"Does that brick belong to this building?" He asked as he pointed to the large red brick that lay in the middle of the floor.

Audrey let out a groan.

Phillip nodded. "I didn't think so. This wasn't an accident. This wasn't some act of God. You've got a problem on your hands, and it came with Gregory Bishop."

"Gregory didn't do this."

"Didn't say he did. I'm well aware of that intern, Audrey. She's missing, and your window is broken. You have a problem."

She knew she had a problem, a big one. She just didn't know how she was supposed to handle it. One thing was for sure. No Walker turned away from a fight. If this was Pepper Dawson who broke her window and sent people stalking her, then Audrey would persevere with her head up. Walkers didn't get taken down.

Lydia came through the back door in a hurried rush. "They cut the line to the cameras."

Phillip and Audrey turned to look at her.

Phillip stepped closer to her. "There's no footage?"

"If I said they cut the line, then no, there's no footage."

"You didn't get a face at the beginning when they cut it?"

"You can't make anything out of it."

"Take me to see it. I'm gonna need to take the tapes too."

Lydia snarled at Phillip. "Fine. But make it fast."

Lydia walked out of the salon, and Phillip turned back to Audrey. "Call your employee and clients, let them know you're closed. Lydia was going to call her brother to help you clean up. Make sure the dog doesn't get hurt. I'll send a car by every half hour, and you stay with someone." Audrey took a breath to argue, and Phillip shot up his hand to stop her. "Don't give me your heroic female crap either. You damn well enough can take care of yourself, and I know that. But I'm not taking any risks," he said as he turned and walked out of the salon.

Audrey looked around the room at the mess that had been created. Suddenly the pain of it squeezed her heart. Whoever had done this, it was like a fist in the gut, and she was sure that's what they were going for. Well, it wasn't going to stop her. Even if that damn window was boarded up tomorrow, she'd be open. Yeah, Walker spirit. She wasn't going to get frazzled by this.

29

Once the glass had been cleaned up, and the window boarded up, Audrey went about rescheduling her and Nichole's day. They'd be in full swing by tomorrow.

Audrey and Black Sabbath walked down to the deli and brought back lunch for her and Lydia. They sat in the grand reception area, at a table that was set up on the dance floor.

Lydia unwrapped her sandwich. "I can't believe somebody would do that to you."

"I'm not going to take it personally. I guess one thing I've learned is that people that are crazy... are just crazy. Their motives aren't normal," she said as she opened her sandwich and slipped Black Sabbath a piece of it.

"You know what would grind salt in their wound? You need to have your grand opening party. We need to move it up. What says screw you better than to fix the window, and have a party."

Audrey laughed as she opened her bottle of water. "I like that idea. Yeah, it says screw you just fine."

"Okay then, we get to work." Lydia took a bite of her sandwich. "You know what? Why don't we make it an event for the entire *Bridal Mecca*? Maybe we could have a sidewalk sale. We'll get some media attention, but will emphasize your salon."

The smile that tugged at Audrey's mouth nearly hurt it was so wide. "This is why you are so fantastic at business. You think big, and you do big."

Lydia lifted her hand to her shoulder and patted herself. "I am pretty good, aren't I?"

Audrey lifted her sandwich to her mouth. "I assume that's why Phillip Smythe is so in love with you." She took the bite.

Lydia held up a finger, and her mouth went tight. "Phillip Smythe is an asshole. And if he is sweet on me, then it's all one-sided. I will never, ever, have anything to do with that man."

Audrey, like most of Lydia's friends, had no idea why the woman hated him so much. But she was adamant about it. Audrey would let it lie, for a while. But she was pretty sure Phillip wasn't done trying to impress Lydia.

FOR THE NEXT TWO WEEKS, preparations for the grandest party ever, according to Lydia, came to the forefront of everyone's mind. Audrey was thankful for the distraction. Gregory was needed on set seven days a week, and nearly fourteen hours a day.

Black Sabbath stayed with her at the salon, which was in normal operation mode. Nichole, as promised, was a huge asset. Her books had been nearly full within a week and a half. She was a marketing genius. Audrey thought that could only be a benefit. Then, she wondered what would happen if Nichole and Lydia got together on a project. The thought made her laugh aloud, and Nichole looked up from her client. Audrey just shook her head and went back to wrapping up a perm for a client she'd had since Audrey was a teenager.

There had been no sign of Pepper Dawson. Audrey had grown accustomed to photographers around every corner, and Gregory made sure there was some security detail around her at all times. Even if it was somebody named Walker.

Phillip checked in with her at least twice a day. He assured her as long as the movie crew was in town, he would do so.

Then, he dropped by three times a day. She finally got smart to it and asked him why.

"The family of Pepper Dawson has issued a missing persons report. She never got on that plane that the production company scheduled her on. She was never picked up at the airport in LA. And as soon as her rent was late, the landlord started looking for her."

"Missing? I think she's some kind of troublemaker. Don't you suppose she ran off with somebody else? Obviously, Gregory was done with her."

Phillip shrugged. "I never know what to think until something else comes about. Therefore, I hang around a little more."

"It's a good thing everybody in this town knows you. I'd start getting worried if I were one of my customers."

"I understand that. But nothing is happening to you on my watch."

For that, she was grateful. She certainly would like to get back to life as it was. However, as long as she was in a relationship with Gregory Bishop, that wasn't going to happen.

They'd been having some long conversations about what would happen when the movie wrapped up in a couple of weeks He was going to have to fly to Hawaii soon after. And then, there was post-production in LA.

Audrey wasn't sure how she was supposed to wrap her head around it. The smart thing would be to say goodbye to him and let him go his way. But over the past month, she'd fallen in love with him.

She had yet to share the words, but he had. It made her too nervous to think of forever with someone who wouldn't be around always. It was stupid. She knew that. Her heart, however, just couldn't accept it yet.

That night, she laid in Gregory's arms in his hotel room, she lifted herself up on her elbow and looked down at him, his eyes heavy and ready to sleep.

"Phillip filled me in on a few things today. You haven't mentioned it, so I'm going to assume you didn't hear, and that you're not hiding it from me."

She saw him tighten his jaw, as he ran a hand down the length of her hair. "He told you that Pepper Dawson is missing."

"So you did know. Didn't you think I might want to know?"

"I'm sure we found out at the same time. I just didn't want to ruin the small time we had with talk of her."

"It seems as though we've dived into a complete relationship. I think the time of keeping secrets is over."

"Agreed." Gregory shifted position so that she was laying down and now he hovered over her. "As soon as we wrap filming, I want you to go away with me."

"I thought you had to leave for Hawaii."

"I'll have a week or so."

She looked up into those dark eyes, so tired. "I don't think it's wise for me to take off any time. I just got my business going."

"And I think Nichole could handle it for a few days."

Curiosity had her. "Where are you taking me?"

A smile inched up from the corners of his lips. "Only to paradise, baby. I'm taking you home to Nebraska."

Audrey wrapped her arms and legs around Gregory and spun him over onto his back. Straddling his body, she looked down at him. "I sincerely thought you were more romantic than that."

"Then I had you fooled. I'm absolutely not."

But she knew better. In the short month they'd been together, they'd gone through highs and lows. He'd proven he was romantic when he'd bought her that beautiful dress, and took her to dinner the day after he met her. How many stories started like theirs?

"Okay, I'll go with you to Nebraska. You're going to have to find something there to impress me. You forget, my name is on one of the biggest ranches in this part of Georgia."

He reached his hand to her cheek and caressed gently. "For the rest of my life, I promise to impress you."

30

Gregory had fallen asleep after they made love. Audrey, however, couldn't sleep at all. *For the rest of my life, I promise to impress you.* His words rang in her ears over and over again. Did he plan to take her back home to meet his family because he had bigger plans for them? What then? He said he'd see that he fit into Georgia, but could he do that? Could he give up living where all the action was for his career?

She supposed people lived everywhere, as long as they had the right connections, they could still work.

Was she ready for this bigger commitment? She thought of Pearl, Bethany, and Jake. Each of them had found love. Hadn't Pearl and Jake both found love in an adversary? And she and Bethany in the creative-minded genius that was Gregory and Kent.

And there it was. She had just boxed them altogether. They were all in love, and so was she.

Looking at the clock on the nightstand, she realized it was two o'clock in the morning. The car would be there for Gregory at six. She didn't want to wake him but, she felt as though she needed to.

Running a finger down his arm gently, he began to stir.

A few moments later, one of his eyes opened and then the other. "Are you okay? What's the matter? Does the dog need to go out?"

Audrey chuckled. "I need to talk to you. I need to tell you something."

"Can it wait until tomorrow?"

"It should never have waited this long."

Gregory rubbed his eyes, then rolled and turned the light on next to him. The room flooded with the glow, and the dog woke up and paced in a circle before laying back down and going back to sleep.

"What's bothering you?"

She smiled. "It bothers me that it has taken me this long to decide that you need to know that I love you."

His eyes opened wider, then he blinked them and opened them again. "Well, okay. That's worth waking me up for." He brushed his fingers over her cheek and pulled her in for a tender kiss. "I love you, too."

Her entire body filled with the warmth that could only have been construed as happiness, because someone loved her. It was time to stop being so negative, and move forward. They would figure this out. It was fate that he had been cast in Kent's movie. It was fate they filmed in Georgia. And it was even fate that he had gone off to Las Vegas with Pepper. Without all that, she wouldn't be in his arms right now.

THE INVITATIONS for the grand opening had been mailed out, responses were pouring in, and everyone had spent an evening at Susan's helping finalize the catering since she was already far enough in her pregnancy to make it uncomfortable to stand that long.

With the party only a day away, Nichole and Audrey worked tirelessly to get the salon ready.

The windows and the mirrors sparkled. Flower arrangements had been set at the door. And at the back was a table which Gia set up, with samples of every product they carried.

When the door to the salon opened, and a delivery driver walked in, Audrey wondered what she had forgotten. They had cleared their books so that nothing would get messed up before the party on Saturday.

The man handed her a box, and she signed for it.

"Oh, what did you get?" Nichole asked as she hurried toward the counter to watch her open the box, as the man let himself out of the salon.

"I have no idea. We didn't order anything. We're stocked."

"Well, get to it." Nichole handed her a pair of scissors.

Audrey cut through the tape and opened the box. Inside, was a shoe box. "I didn't order..."

She lifted the box out of the other box. Boldly, on the side of the box was written; Jimmy Choo.

Nichole gasped. "You can afford Jimmy Choo shoes?"

Audrey laughed. "Hell no." She smiled widely. "This is a thoughtful gift a month in the making." Pulling out one of the designer shoes, she studied it. Would he ever not amaze her?

Audrey put the shoe back in the box.

"Aren't you going to put them on?" Nichole asked.

Audrey shook her head. "We're done here aren't we?"

"Sure. Everything is set."

"Good. I will wear them. And he will be glad I did."

Nichole gave her a roaring cheer, and hurried her out the door.

GREGORY MANAGED his way from the elevator to the door and pushed it open. He was exhausted. They'd filmed the scene that came after the spaceship's crash, the battle scene. So he looked like hell anyway. He'd been covered in blood and dirt for fourteen hours. He'd been pushed to the ground at least twenty times. That foam rock, which they pushed him up against, had a sharp spot that went right into his back. The guy, whom he'd been training with all month, missed four times with the sword that went right into his arm. Thank goodness it was a prop. Had it actually been a taser sword, he would've lost his arm.

The fight scenes were brutal enough, he thought. But getting all that damn blood off his face, that was equally brutal.

He'd never say it out loud, but he certainly could use a few facials at Audrey's salon when this was all done.

For right now, all he wanted to do was relax in a hot tub.

He dropped his bag on the couch and realized how quiet it was. They had agreed to meet at the hotel, right? Right then, Black Sabbath sauntered through the living room. He looked up at him, considered for a moment, and then went to him. He snuggled up to his legs as if he were hugging him. Always a sight for sore eyes, Gregory appreciated him. He knelt down and gave him a proper hug.

"Where is our girl?"

As if the dog understood the question, he started toward the bedroom and Gregory followed.

Standing in the doorway, he took in the sight. Audrey laid on the bed completely naked and asleep. She'd pulled the sheet over her shoulders, leaving everything else exposed. And on her feet, were the new Jimmy Choo shoes.

It gave him great pleasure to see her there. It was obvious she was trying to surprise him. Had that blood come off quicker, he'd have been home an hour earlier.

Kicking off his shoes, he walked to her as he pulled off his shirt. Audrey stirred as he sat down on the bed next to her.

"Were you waiting for me?" He asked as he trailed a finger up the outside of her thigh.

"I was trying. What time is it?"

"Eleven. Did you get some new shoes?"

Audrey nodded, her eyes drifting closed again. Then, her eyes shot open. She sat up in bed nearly hitting heads with him. "I thought you bought me the shoes. Didn't you buy me shoes?"

Panic had filled her voice, and he didn't much like it. "Of course I did. Who else would buy you Jimmy Choo shoes that match the dress I bought you?"

She rested her hand on her chest and lay back down. "I don't know. There's just so much in my head right now. The party. The broken window. Phillip telling me Pepper is missing."

"That shouldn't be bothering you."

"Of course it bothers me. She threw that brick through my front window and..."

"We don't know that."

"My gut knows it." Audrey sat up, pulling the sheet over her, to his dismay. "I'll just feel better when she surfaces."

"I'm sure she will. And we're going to keep going on with our life as planned." Gregory pulled the sheet down. "Were you sleeping and not trying to seduce me?"

The smile that formed on Audrey's beautiful lips answered the question for him. She raised her hand up around his neck and pulled him down on top of her.

That was where the conversation ended. The rest of the night would be all about forgetting everything outside that door.

31

The phone ringing on the nightstand brought Audrey straight up in bed. Gregory came out of the bathroom brushing his teeth. He mumbled, "It's your phone."

Audrey fumbled to come to her senses. She reached for the phone, and answered it. "Hello?"

"It's Phillip," the voice said on the other end. She tried to put it all together, and a moment later she came to enough to realize exactly who Phillip was.

"What's wrong? Why are you calling me this early? Something happened. Who's hurt?"

"Calm down, calm down. We have a problem. Nobody is hurt. Can you get to your house?"

Gregory moved to the bed and sat down. She stared silently. Then Phillip repeated the question, and she took a breath. "Yes. What happened?"

"Just head this way."

The call disconnected, and Audrey dropped the phone.

Gregory gathered her hands, they shook. "What's going on?" He asked in a calm tone.

"Phillip needs me at my house. He didn't say why."

Gregory nodded, then stood. "I'll call and let them know I'm going to be late. I'll drive you to your house."

She agreed. Everything imaginable went through her brain. Why her house? What could have happened? She supposed that was what Phillip wanted to tell her. But he wanted to tell her in person. That always made it worse.

GREGORY PULLED up in front of Audrey's house and parked behind Phillip's cruiser. There were two more cruisers on either end of the street. He gave her hand a squeeze before he stepped out of the car and Phillip opened her door.

Audrey looked up at the house as she stepped out of the car. "What happened?"

"It looks like someone broke in. One of your neighbors called around four to say that there was some ruckus, and that she was sure you weren't here. They found forced entry. The glass back door has been broken."

Gregory moved in next, put an arm around her shoulders. "Can she go in and look?"

"That's what we want to do. We don't think anything is missing or destroyed. But it's obvious somebody was in there. Some drawers were open and a couple of cabinets."

Audrey couldn't think of a thing she kept anywhere that would be of any use to anyone. Perhaps a few pieces of jewelry, but she didn't keep many things of value. "I'll look around."

Gregory escorted her to the house with his arm around her. The door was already open.

Carefully, she stepped inside. Her heart ached to think that somebody violated her personal space. What could somebody want with her? In her mind, there was one person who seemed to be vengeful against her. Had they found Pepper Dawson?

She saw glass scattered on the floor. She stepped carefully

over it and walked toward her bedroom. Inside the room, drawers had been opened and their contents tossed around.

"I didn't keep anything in my drawers," she said as Phillip walked in the room.

"What about the kitchen cupboards?"

Audrey thought. "Kitchenware. Maybe a few bottles of wine." She tried to mentally walk through all the cupboards of her kitchen. What else was there but food and dishes? She sucked in her breath. "My extra set of keys are there. Keys to my salon, Pearl's bridal salon, and a few keys to ranch vehicles."

Phillip gave her a slow nod. "Go and see if they're there. If not, we might've found what they were after."

Audrey and Gregory quickly maneuvered past the broken glass to the kitchen. The weight of the anxiety was heavy in her belly. "They're gone," she said as she felt around with her hand in the cupboard.

"I'm going to send somebody to the salon. Call Nichole and tell her…"

Audrey's phone rang, and she pulled it from her pocket. "It's Lydia," she said as she answered the phone. She listened to Lydia's hysterical banter on the other end and disconnected. She looked up at both Phillip and Gregory. Tears were already rising in her throat and welling in her eyes.

Gregory stepped toward her and took her hand. "Take a couple of breaths."

Audrey closed her eyes and did just as he said. Then, as she opened her eyes, she looked toward Phillip. "Somebody broke into the salon." Her heart thumped in her chest, and her breathing became labored. "They threw red paint on everything. They ruined my salon."

Gregory pulled her into his arms and held her tightly. The flood of tears now broke through. Everything she worked for was ruined, according to Lydia. Now what?

Phillip moved to them. "I'll get somebody there. Let's head over."

Audrey nodded. All she could think about now was trying to rebuild. What about Nichole? She had a family to take care of.

Gregory kept his arm around her and walked to the car. Once she was inside, he closed the door and walked around.

"I'm not going to say it will be alright. I know this is something that we all have to get through."

Her anger boiled to the point of explosion. "This is all because I got involved with you. All because you showed up that night and swept me off my feet. Everything was going to be perfect. Everything. Now because you slept with some crazy bitch, my life is ruined."

GREGORY REMAINED quiet throughout the drive. He understood her anger. He was angry too. However, he didn't believe that she blamed him deep down in her heart. He let her be angry. Hell, he'd give her space if that's what she needed. But he wasn't going to give up. He had never felt like this before, and he wasn't going to let her go. But she needed her space. He understood that.

There were already multiple police cruisers at the salon by the time they arrived. Lydia hurried toward the car as Audrey climbed from the other side. Gregory stepped back and let them mourn together. Nichole ran down the street toward them. She too enveloped them in a hug, and the three women held each other.

That was when Gregory's phone buzzed in his pocket. It was his manager, and at the moment the last person he wanted to talk to. He strolled down the street just a bit as he answered the phone.

His manager's voice was nearly as frantic as he had heard Lydia's through the phone when she had called Audrey. He stopped with his back turned to the crowd behind him, and listened to his manager.

New photos had been released. It seemed as though his getaway, which had been hijacked by Pepper Dawson, was about to go even more public. His manager told him about the details they received in a letter. Gregory Bishop was about to become a victim of blackmail, and he couldn't see any way around it.

He tucked his phone back in his pocket the moment that his manager hung up. He was torn as to what to do. After what she'd said, he was sure that Audrey didn't want him around. His manager wanted him to meet and discuss a strategy to deal with the media. And yet, he wanted to stay by her side. Who gave a damn what happened to his reputation at this point. Audrey's entire livelihood was at stake. He owed her the respect to get her salon back together as quickly as possible. Her party was the next day.

Suddenly he had a mission, enough people, and money to make it happen. Audrey's salon would be back open for business, and the party would go on as planned. He'd see to that.

32

Gregory ignored the pleas from his manager to head to the set. Even Bethany was helping to dodge calls from the production crew.

Everybody who had been part of building the salon had started to come by. One by one Gregory met every one of her relatives. He kept himself in the background, as it was evident Audrey was too distraught to have him around. She blamed him. That was fine.

He spent the morning making phone calls. As soon as Phillip released the site for cleanup, he had a crew.

As lunchtime rolled around, and others showed up, Gregory ordered lunch to be delivered to the reception hall. He helped them set up a few tables, and they served lunch to everybody.

Relief that so many people had come to help Audrey put her salon back together washed over her face, but the anguish was still there. He pulled a bottle of water from a Styrofoam cooler, which he ordered as well, and took it to her.

"You look like you could use a little more water," he offered as he sat down next to her. "And I know you blame me for this, so I'll make this very short."

She lifted her hand and rested it on top of his. "That was wrong for me to say. I was angry, and I needed a reason. It was reason enough somebody messed up my house and now has messed with my salon, twice. But it wasn't fair for me to pin that on you."

"Strangely enough it makes sense, because I love you, and because you love me," he reminded her. "While you've been dealing with Phillip and the legalities, I've been putting a few things into motion. Your party is tomorrow."

Audrey dipped her head into the palms of her hands and ran her fingers through her hair. "I'm sure the news'll get around quick enough, there's not going to be any party. There is no..."

Gregory held up his hand as if to stop her. "The party is on."

Audrey raised her head and looked at him. "You saw it in there. Everything is covered in red paint. It's ruined. I put every dime I had into there, I don't know how I can rebuild."

"I already have a crew mobilized. If they can do home improvement shows where they remodel an entire home in a week, we can clean up the salon by tomorrow night."

"How?"

"Let me deal with it. It's a fantastic opportunity to use my fame for good instead of bad. I already have a truck headed to pick up new equipment. There is a cleaning crew coming to try and get the paint off the floor. Russell is headed to buy paint for the walls. And we have a crew of about fifty ready to pull an all-nighter."

Audrey stared at him through stunned eyes. "Why are you doing that?"

"I told you. I love you. And you know what, I do think that it's part my fault. There's a lot of attention on you that you didn't ask for. Perhaps I have to do this to clear my conscience."

"I don't know what to say."

He lifted her hand to his lips and kissed her palm. "Say you love me. Say you'll stay with me when things get tough," he said, because he knew things were going to get tough.

"I do love you. Thank you," she said, as Nichole signaled for her. "I'll be back."

Gregory watched her leave the room, and he sat there alone for a moment. At some point, he would have to deal with the crisis at hand for himself. He didn't know what kind of photos Pepper had. Anything was unauthorized, that was for sure. He hadn't invited her to Las Vegas. She just happened to be there when he arrived. Yes, he was stupid enough to let it turn into something. He was probably careless enough, too, that anything could have happened. There was no assurance that whatever came out, whatever was leaked to the press, wouldn't devastate his relationship with Audrey. He didn't want that. All he wanted was her, and now he knew he wanted her for the rest of his life. But how could he convince her of that? The business she had worked so hard for, and invested everything in, was in shambles. She had a reputation in the town, and hadn't she said she was from the wrong side of the Walker family?

Gregory looked around the room and realized that he had never seen her father show up. He didn't like that either.

At this point, all he could hope for was that his love could be enough. Moment to moment, he thought. He'd take care of this. And he'd fight for her even if they had nothing left in the end.

AUDREY WATCHED in surprise as her family, all of them, and people from the movie crew began to clean her salon. Ruined equipment was taken out. The floors were being taken care of, and Russell and his crew of brothers were painting her walls. She could cry, she thought. This was what family was all about, showing up when someone needed help. The obvious person missing, of course, was her father. He didn't get it. He never got it.

None of that mattered really. She had all these other people there.

Susan, obviously too pregnant to do manual labor, had set up a sandwich buffet for dinner. Russell's wife, Chelsea, also too pregnant to do manual labor, sat in Lydia's reception hall with her mother-in-law making beautiful baskets to give away at the grand opening. Audrey now owed her business to the local beauty supply place. They had donated all of the samples and all of the gifts to replace the ruined ones.

Gregory moved in behind her and wrapped his arms around her waist. "You have quite a community here."

Audrey smiled. "We do," she said as she turned to face him. "Thank you. None of this would have started without you. Maybe in time, but not tonight. I love you."

He gently pressed a kiss to her lips. "That's payment enough. Listen," he began, "I need to go meet my manager. I don't know how long I'll be. This is going to go on all night, and I'll be back."

"I hope they don't fire you over this. You took a whole day to be here. I hope they see how gracious you are."

"It's not about that. I'll explain later." He kissed her again and headed out the back door.

Bethany, covered in paint, moved to her and handed her a paintbrush. "I know it's a little bit overwhelming, but I certainly could use some help with the shampoo area."

Audrey took the paintbrush and kissed her sister on the cheek. "I love him."

Bethany grinned. "There's not a person in this building who doesn't know that. He's got a good heart, Audrey. Kent likes him too, and you know he's a good judge of character."

Audrey did know that. She also remembered that Kent had warned her against him. Well, not against him, but had warned her. Maybe there was more to it. Maybe it was because he knew something like this would happen.

Well, she looked around at all the Walkers working so hard for her benefit, she knew that whoever did this had to be disappointed. They weren't going to hurt Gregory, and they weren't going to hurt her. Love and family were stronger than hate.

33

Gregory's manager, Leo Frost, was waiting for him in the lobby of his hotel. He stood as Gregory walked through the door.

"You're a pain in my ass, Bishop," he said as he hurriedly walked, matching Gregory's pace as they headed toward the elevator. "Why do people keep hiring you?"

"Because I'm the best at what I do. I'm not as big an ass as the world makes me out to be, and I'm sexy."

That had Leo laughing as they stepped onto the elevator and headed to Gregory's room.

"This is a huge mess you're in. You know that?"

Gregory nodded. "It shouldn't be a mess. I spent two nights with the woman. I don't have a relationship with her. I made a mistake. Now she's going to kill someone if we don't stop her."

As they exited the elevator, Leo slowed, causing Gregory to turn to him.

Leo scratched the stubble on his cheek. "You think that Pepper Dawson did all of this?"

"Yes," he answered adamantly. "She's jealous of my relationship with Audrey. I went from her to another woman, and she can't stand it. She broke Audrey's front window, broke into her house, and now has destroyed her business. She needs to be locked up."

"She's in the pictures with you. She's not the one who took them."

"Then she set someone up to do it. C'mon, this kind of thing happens all the time."

Gregory turned back to his door and unlocked it with the card he pulled from his pocket.

Leo followed him inside and locked the door behind him. "Pepper is missing. You do know that, right? Her family has filed a missing person's report."

"Yep, and don't you suppose she's in hiding?"

Leo shook his head. "No. I think something happened to her. She might be a crazy woman, but I don't think she's this crazy, Greg. I want you to reach out to whoever sent us those photos of you two."

"Don't you think we should turn it over to the authorities?"

"No. I think you should keep this under wraps as much as possible. Greg, if you don't fix this, your career is over."

He didn't believe that for one second. And even if he did, all he had to do was to think about the pain on Audrey's face when she saw her salon to know it didn't matter. If his career brought someone he loved so much pain, it wasn't worth it. He'd been raised a farm boy, he could certainly become one again.

Gregory pulled two bottles of water from the refrigerator and handed Leo one. Just as he took a breath to debate the black-mail, Leo's phone buzzed. Gregory watched the man's face lose color. He set down his water to go to him, just as his own phone buzzed in his pocket.

He pulled it out to see that a photo had been sent from an

anonymous number. "Dear God," he let the words slip as he looked at Leo.

On their phone screens was a photo of Pepper Dawson tied to a chair. Her hair was covering her bloodied face.

"Greg, you're in some serious trouble."

"I didn't do this."

Leo held his phone out closer to him. "That's your trailer on the lot."

His breath caught in his lungs. "Call the police. I'm going to get to Audrey."

Leo only nodded.

Gregory put a hand on his shoulder. "Call the police. Call the set. Get security into my trailer. Hurry."

He left Leo standing in his hotel room staring down at his phone. Certainly, he would come to enough to get some help. As for Gregory, he needed to get to Audrey before anyone else could. This wasn't a crazy fangirl moment anymore. This was a matter of life and death.

Gregory opted for the stairs, instead of the elevator. He handed the valet the tag for his truck, but a few moments later the attendant came back to him.

"Sir, your truck isn't in the lot. Are you sure you left it here?"

At that moment his phone buzzed again in his pocket. And again, there was another photo of Pepper, still bloodied as she was in the first one, and obviously unconscious. This time, however, she was in the seat of Gregory's truck, which he'd purchased from the Walkers.

He raked his fingers through his hair and called Audrey's number.

When she answered, her voice was soft and carefree. He didn't want to put panic in her, but no matter what he said, it would.

"Hey, Phillip isn't there, is he?"

"Phillip? No. He stopped by a little bit ago."

Gregory winced. For the first time, he'd like to have the nosy cop standing there. "Message me his phone number, okay?"

"Gregory, what's wrong?" she asked, and he could hear the hint of worry in her voice.

"Leo wants to talk to him. Movie stuff."

"Okay. I'll send it over," her voice had softened.

He said goodbye, and a moment later the text came through with the phone number. Immediately, as he asked the attendant to get him a taxi, he called Phillip.

AUDREY WAVED to Nichole as she left. The salon was looking fantastic, and she had Gregory to thank for putting it all together. She owed him big now, she thought happily as she moved to the door to lock it.

The red pickup which used to belong to her cousins, and now belonged to Gregory, drove down the street. She waited a moment for him to turn back, but he didn't. Perhaps he was going around the back. She'd find him there.

Just as she clicked the lock, she saw Phillip coming down the street at a hurried pace. Unlocking the door, she opened it for him.

"I'm leaving. You don't have to check up on me now. In fact, Gregory just drove by, so I think he's parking..."

"That wasn't him," Phillip said pushing open the door and locking it behind him. "I just got off the phone with him. His truck was stolen. You're coming with me," he instructed as he walked to the back of the salon, his hand on the butt of his gun.

"What is going on?"

Phillip emerged from the back. "Where's Lydia?"

"At her grandfather's house for dinner. Why she'd put herself in a position to have to put up with the man is beyond..."

"Your employee is gone? Your cousins?"

"All of them. Phillip, you're freaking me out. What's going on?"

"C'mon. I'll tell you in the car."

He waited by the door, watching the street, as she gathered her purse and personal items. She locked the door, and then he nearly pulled her down the street to his cruiser and shoved her inside.

The moment he climbed into the car and started the engine, she had a lot to say to him.

"What are you doing? Am I in trouble? Did I do something wrong? You yanked me out of my salon. Did you see all the work that went into it today? I don't know what your problem is."

"I think you're in danger, and you're not leaving my side, now shut up," he said in his warning tone that still was cool and in control. "I'm taking you out to the ranch."

"The ranch? Seriously, that's forty-five minutes away. I don't need to go out there."

"It's exactly where you need to go, and you're not going to argue with me." He accelerated the car as they edged out of town. "Listen, Gregory is being blackmailed. We don't know by who, but..."

"Oh, I know by who. Geez, what's wrong with that woman?"

"Would you listen?" He snapped out the question as he shifted her a stern look. "He was sent photos of Pepper Dawson. Someone has her. Someone kidnapped her. The photos are being taken in areas that belong to Gregory."

"What do you mean 'areas that belong to Gregory'?"

"I mean they were taken in his trailer, and in the truck that was stolen," he explained. "He sent me the pictures, and she's not in good shape."

"But she's still alive?"

"For now, or so we think. That's why we're taking you out here. Your aunt and uncle are waiting for you. So are your cousins."

She swallowed hard. There was one question she needed answered. "Where is Gregory?"

34

Phillip had alerted Jake as to what was going on. When Gregory had the taxi drop him off at Jake's garage, he and his fiancée Missy were standing outside waiting for him.

"Phillip has her," Jake said as he moved toward him. "He's taking her out to the ranch. Everyone is out there. She's going to be safe."

"Good. They didn't find Pepper in my trailer. In fact, security has no idea how they got there. Perhaps the photos have been doctored."

Missy shook her head. "That means somebody has been in your trailer then."

"Yeah, that's what bugs me."

"My truck is out back," Jake said as they began to walk around the building. "It's a forty-five minute drive through town and out to the ranch." He smiled wide. "Missy and I can get you there in twenty-five."

Missy's smile mimicked her fiancés. "You're not afraid of a little speed are you?"

Gregory shrugged as they approached the truck. "Who, me? I fly spaceships."

AUDREY THOUGHT she might be sick from the speed at which Phillip's cruiser accelerated. She'd never driven those back roads that fast. With each terrifying bump in the road, she gripped her fingers tighter to the side of the door.

"Been driving these roads all my life, just like you have. You can relax," Phillip said. "At least you're not the one driving out with your brother."

"Jake is bringing Gregory?"

"Yeah, I assume they'll get there about the same time we do."

It was then that Phillip's phone rang in his breast pocket. Expertly, he pulled it out and answered.

"This is him. Yeah, headed that way." He let out a long sigh.

He tucked the phone back in his pocket. "Gregory and his manager just got a new picture."

"And?"

He shifted her a look, and she knew she wasn't going to like the answer.

"Your balcony."

Audrey felt her stomach lurch, and she closed her eyes to look away. "I don't understand what's going on."

"Gregory is being blackmailed. Whoever has Dawson, they want him to pay to keep it all quiet. I assume that's the reason for all the personal backgrounds. Those are all places he would take somebody. Probably the places he's been with you."

"And you think if he doesn't pay up, they'll come for me?"

"That's exactly what we think."

"So I'm going to hide out at my family's ranch until you guys find this person? What if it's her? What if she's the one setting all this up? After all, I was in the makeup department. Gregory looked like he was dead."

Phillip nodded as he turned down the road that would take them to the ranch. "We thought of that. We have experts looking at the pictures for trauma. I'm pretty sure we're going to find that she has nothing to do with this. At least this ransom part."

When they pulled up in front of her aunt and uncle's house, her entire family converged on the driveway. It was amazing, she thought, the panic slipped away. The only Walker missing was her father, and Jake, but she'd already been told he had Gregory. Lydia pushed through the crowd of them and headed right to Audrey.

"Nothing is going happen to you. They have to get through all of us first."

Audrey had no words. She pulled Lydia in and hugged her, and then everyone else.

Just as Phillip had said, Jake and Missy pulled up with a white-knuckled Gregory only a few moments later.

He nearly fell out of the truck as soon as it came to a stop.

Audrey broke from her family and ran to him. She wrapped her arms around his neck tightly.

"This person isn't going to hurt us. Nobody is going to let them."

"I know. That's why we're out here." He stepped back and grasped her hands. "I have the helicopter enroute. It'll be here in an hour."

"A helicopter?" she asked. "You're leaving?"

"We're leaving." He raised his hand to her cheek. "Taking you to Nebraska. Whoever that lunatic is, they're in Georgia. Phillip is going to find them. But we are going to get you out of harm's way."

"No. We just got my business back in order. We're having a party tomorrow."

Phillips stepped forward. "We will have that party the moment you get back. There is no reason for anyone to get hurt here."

She looked around at the faces that surrounded them. It was obvious she had been the only one not in on the plan. Resigning to the situation, she took a deep breath. "Someone needs to call Nichole. She's a single mother, and I am her source of income."

Her uncle stepped forward and touched her arm. "She'll be fine. We have your back, Audrey," he said, and she knew because she had looked around, that was a direct statement toward her father, who was missing here, too. It was then she realized that she did come to the right side of the Walker family, and he had isolated himself from it.

Audrey looked back at Gregory. "Okay, I trust you, and I don't want you hurt."

"And I love you, and I don't want you hurt either."

Just as Gregory had said, the helicopter arrived behind the house an hour later. Phillip had already mobilized people to Audrey's house, and they had found nobody there. He set somebody in motion to be waiting at her salon, or anywhere around the *Bridal Mecca*. It was the next logical choice of where they would take her.

Gregory and Audrey climbed into the helicopter. He, seemed to be at ease, while she was scared to death.

"You're taking me home?"

He smiled. "Yes, I'm taking you to our farm. My dad can't wait to meet you."

Audrey shook her head. "I'm sure this isn't what he had in mind for meeting me."

Gregory took her hand and squeezed it. "He doesn't care

about the circumstance, though he's very worried about you. He knows how I feel about you, and he's excited to have you in his home."

The helicopter took them to Atlanta, where a private jet waited for them. Though Audrey was running from a lunatic, and this was to save her life, she couldn't help but have a little excitement for all the new things she was experiencing.

As soon as they landed in Nebraska, the man started toward them. She didn't need to be introduced. She knew the man was his father.

Gregory moved to him and wrapped his arms around him.

"Thanks for being here," Gregory said.

"Thanks for thinking to come this way," the man said before he turned to her. "You must be Audrey."

She held out her hand. "Yes, I am."

"George Bishop," he said as he shook her hand. "Nice to meet the woman my son loves."

Audrey sighed. She wasn't quite sure how to handle him having that knowledge.

Gregory slipped his arm around her waist and kissed her cheek. "I tell him everything. No secrets kept."

AUDREY SAT in the backseat of George Bishop's truck, and they drove from the airport out to the farm where Gregory had grown up. Through the window, she watched the miles of fields pass, and thought of how it reminded her of home. It was funny she thought, she and Gregory came from such different lives, but their beginnings were similar.

She didn't look at him as a movie star anymore, she thought as she listened to him converse with his father. He was just a man. A man whose job put him in the spotlight. Just as her sister was just a woman, and not some faded Hollywood star.

And when this was all done, she knew, there might be a happily ever after. No man goes through something like this for a woman, without loving her a great deal. She put her hand to her chest to ease her racing heart. She'd never been around true love firsthand. Well, she rethought that. She'd been around her aunt and uncle her whole life and her cousins as they fell in love. And even her sister and brother as they found true love, she'd watched it blossom. But she hadn't been raised around it.

It was no surprise that it took her a while to recognize it. But she certainly wasn't going to let it pass her by.

35

The homestead where Gregory's father lived, had been in their family for generations. And it, much like the fields they passed through to get there, felt like home to Audrey.

Horses ran in one pasture and crops grew in another. The barn was as big as the one just beyond Eric's house and painted bright red. The house was small, but who needed a big house when they had such a beautiful view around them?

As they climbed from the truck and started toward the house, Gregory slipped his arm around her waist and pulled her close. "Well, what do you think?"

"I think it's fantastic. It makes me appreciate you just a little bit more, knowing that you grew from humble ground."

"I told you we have a lot in common."

They settled into the house, in the room where Gregory grew up. His father set out to start dinner, and Audrey checked in with her sisters.

There had been no commotion since they had left. But Phillip had them all on high alert.

It had been decided that Nichole would keep the salon open,

but there would be somebody there with her at all times. Phillip had taken this case personally and was going to be sure he was in the salon nearly every hour.

"And he wants you to keep alert too. He says the movie set is abuzz over where Gregory disappeared to," Pearl informed her. "So don't get too comfortable. Keep your eyes open."

"I will," she promised.

When she finished her phone calls with her sisters, Gregory sat down on the bed next to her. "No one will find you here. Leo is on the set, and so is Kent. They have their ears open. Phillip and his crew are going to find Pepper, and when they do, she will lead them to the person that is sending those photos. It won't be long."

"I don't know how you deal with all of this. Why do you want to put yourself in a position where people can get to you like this?"

Gregory grinned as he took her hand and pressed a kiss to her fingers. "How can you touch somebody you've never met? I mean, somebody walks in and wants a haircut? You have to touch them. You have to intimately get near them. Why would anybody want to do that?"

Ah, so he answered her question with his own. "I guess we both love what we do too much to notice how intimate we get with people."

"I don't belittle what you do. The world wants to look good. Everybody needs to feel like they get put back together, and you do that. You lend them an open ear. And well, hell, you are just very pleasant to be around."

Audrey smiled. She appreciated people that understood what she did. She had fought that her entire life, starting with her father assuming that hair stylists were uneducated workers.

"What's going to happen to the movie? You're a vital part of that. You can't just leave."

"There are ways around that. There are plenty of scenes that need my stunt double and not me. Besides, they understand that me being alive is as important as being there."

"So they're as worried about you as my family is about me?"

"Of course. Most of them know her, and half of them think she's part of this."

"So what made you take off with her?" she asked, because she had to know.

Gregory rubbed his fingertips across his forehead and took a moment to gather his thoughts. Then, he looked her in the eye and took her hand again. "I didn't plan it. In fact, I planned to just have a weekend to myself. Do whatever I wanted to. She just happened to be there. I can't say I took advantage of her, as much as we took advantage of each other. It wasn't anything special. And in hindsight, it was the stupidest thing I've ever done. Like I said before, Hollywood gets in your head."

"That statement scares me more than you know, especially now that I love you."

"I'm not a man to take that lightly, Audrey. I don't just say those words to anyone, and I certainly don't accept them from just anyone. But I accept them from you—I know you mean them. This is different, I swear. I might have to prove that to you all over again, and I will if I have to. I have found my soulmate. I can't imagine there's anyone else out there that I want to spend my life with. If you walked out on me over this today, I'd be broken. I'm quite sure I want to spend the rest of my life with you."

Audrey felt the tears stinging her throat. "I'm not sure we're being wise about this. In a little over a month, you said I love you, and you're making statements like that. Does anybody really know love that quickly?"

He lifted his hand to her face and gently brushed his thumb

over her cheek. "Don't forget, you said you loved me too. You did mean it, didn't you?"

"Yes," she said quickly. "I've never felt like I feel with you. I guess you can fall in love that quickly," she sighed as she understood it herself. "You're right. When I think about the future, I think of you in it."

"And that's why I have you here, hiding in my childhood bedroom." He laughed as he looked around the room. "I would die if anything happened to you. And here, it won't. So, until they find the lunatic, you're safe here."

"With you?"

Gregory pressed a kiss to her lips. "Always with me. I promise you that."

For two days, there had been no word. Phillip had kept his promise to be at the salon every hour. Nichole worked just as she said she would. Each of the Walker family spent some part of the day in town at the *Bridal Mecca*, keeping an eye on one another.

Audrey's phone rang all day long. Each of her siblings, and her cousins, calling to check on her. It indeed brought a great sense of Walker spirit to her heart.

She quite enjoyed watching Gregory jump into farm life with his father. She'd never seen anyone sexier on a tractor.

And while he helped out with regular chores, she was able to explore a bit.

The barn was one of her favorite places to relax, and take in the silence.

She tended to the horses, even making friends with a young colt named Sam. It made her think of the plot of land that was promised to her. She'd never thought much of it, but now, perhaps she would like to build on it—with Gregory.

Audrey ran a brush over the young colt. She'd spent most of her day with him, as Gregory and his father were tending to the field.

She decided he was going to be a wise horse, as when she spoke to him, it seemed as though he answered. Audrey laughed at the thought.

If she did build on the Walker land, as some of her cousins had and her brother would, she could have her own horse, her own garden, and chickens. On another solitary laugh, she decided she definitely wanted chickens.

She finished up grooming the horse, and she heard the sound of the truck pulling up outside. Gregory and his father must be done in the field, she thought. Suddenly, she was very anxious to tell Gregory about her desire to have chickens.

Audrey put away the brush and went back to tell the horse goodbye.

"I'll be back with a treat for you later," she promised as she headed out of the barn.

36

Audrey walked out into the sunshine and enjoyed the feel of it on her skin. She looked around but didn't see a truck. Perhaps she had just thought she heard something.

She walked to the front porch of the house and looked out into the field. There, she could still see the tractor and the faint figures of the two men working on an irrigator.

She wondered, could Gregory give it all up to return to something so simple? The thought of it gave her heart a little buzz. If they thought they could have a life together, she would have to be very secure in herself. After all, the reason they were there was that he had let himself be too Hollywood, as he had said. But she believed him when he said it wasn't like that with her.

Audrey sat in one of the rocking chairs on the wraparound porch and leaned her head back. She supposed it would become old hat, just as it was for her to take on clients. She might get to travel to exotic places and be on set with him. Then again, perhaps it would be like he was just going to work, and she would go in and work her job as well. It wasn't as if they would be the only people in the world where one of them had to travel often for work.

She closed her eyes for a moment and let herself relax in the quiet. But then she heard the horses from behind the barn. She lifted her head and looked around. They weren't settling.

Audrey walked toward the side of the barn and could see the horses in the pen running in circles. Something had spooked them.

Gathering a large stick on the side of the house, she hurried toward the horses. Was the weather changing? Perhaps a snake had gotten through the grass. But when she turned the corner, she saw what had startled them.

The truck her cousin had sold to Gregory sat at the back of the barn. She felt her hands shaking at her side, and she gripped the stick tighter. Her breath was harder to push to her lungs, and her heart raced in her chest.

Moving toward the truck, she saw that the passenger door was open and there was a trail of blood on the seat.

The horses continued to battle the confined space in which they were held. What had they seen, she wondered as she noticed the back door to the barn was slightly open.

Audrey pulled her phone from her pocket. She had to alert Gregory.

Inside the barn, she could hear rustling, though she wasn't sure if it was a horse or a person. Looking down at her phone she hit Gregory's contact, and press the button to call just as she felt the sharp pain of being hit with something across her back.

Audrey hit the ground, her phone flying several feet in front of her. Her stomach roiled at the pain, and her head spun.

She could hear footsteps behind her, and she fought her own body to turn over. Then just as she managed to, her vision blurred from the hit she had taken, someone grabbed her feet and began to pull her.

The rocks scraped her back and her head, and she tried to will herself to break free, but the man who had hold of her was simply stronger.

He dragged her into the nearest stall and let her feet fall right near the battered body of Pepper Dawson.

Audrey could smell the blood and sweat from the woman next to her. She wasn't sure Pepper was alive, but she had to hope that she was. Because if she was, it meant Audrey might be able to talk her way out of whatever might happen next.

She blinked her eyes to try and focus as she felt the kick to her side. Realizing she was too weak even to scream, she tried to breathe in through her nose and clear her mind. She needed to try and focus on the man who stood before her.

"Who are you?" she managed weakly.

"Shut up."

She saw that he had something in his hand. It was small, but it wasn't a gun. That had been what she was most fearful of, being shot.

Blinking again, she realized it was a camera.

He was taking pictures of the two of them slumped in the hay. This had to be the man who had blackmailed Gregory.

She lifted her focus from the camera to the man's face, and she recognized him.

"I've met you before. You came into my salon."

He continued to take pictures and ignore her. "You said you were a photographer on the set." She swallowed hard as her throat began to burn. "Nobody knew who you were."

He moved closer to both of them, moving the hair from Pepper's battered face. Audrey noticed the slightest bit of movement from her and realized she was indeed alive.

The man focused the camera on Audrey, who managed her hand to her face. It was then she felt his fist at her jaw, and she fell over on her side.

"Move again, and I'll kill you," the man growled as he took more pictures.

Audrey could feel her consciousness begin to slip from her. The world spun and her vision grew dark. She tried to return her gaze to him, willing herself not to blackout. She had to make a move on the man. Her back burned from where he'd hit her, her legs ached from where he had dragged her, her jaw throbbed with immense pain. But she wasn't going to let him kill her. Whoever this man was, he was going to pay for what he had done.

She tried to map out the barn in her head. Then she realized she could hear movement next to them. Sam's stall was right there. Could she somehow get the horse to distract the man?

She thought about the day she'd met the horse. When she rubbed him down, she had whistled, and he had whinnied along with her. At the time she thought it was quite a clever trick, now she wondered if he could save her life.

As the man fidgeted with his camera, Audrey licked her lips and tried to make her mouth as moist as she could. There would be only one shot to make a noise.

She sucked in a breath, and whistled as loudly as she could. The horse replied just as she hoped he would, and the man looked to his side.

With every ounce of energy she possibly could find, and from her seated position, she charged at the man's legs knocking him backward.

37

G regory stared down at his phone. Nobody was on the other end of the line, but he could hear a noise.

"Audrey? Honey pick up your phone," he called out to her.

"What's going on," his father asked.

"I don't know. I can hear her moving around, but it's muffled. I thought I could hear people talking, but she's not there."

His father dropped the tools in the back of the truck and opened the door. "Maybe she's talking to that person that came up the road a bit ago. I thought they went the other way but..."

Gregory pulled open the door to the truck and started the engine. "Get in," he instructed his father. "What did the vehicle look like, that came up the road?"

"Red pickup truck. Million of them out this way," his father said as he slammed the door and Gregory quickly took off. "You think she's in trouble?"

"I bought a red pickup truck off her cousins. Whoever took that woman, stole it. I do think she's in trouble."

Gregory drove out of the field as quickly as he could, his father's old pickup truck barely holding together as he maneuvered over ruts and rocks. As he came up to the road to the house, he gunned it a little faster.

It was then that he saw the pickup parked at the back of the barn. "Son-of-a-bitch!" He hollered as he came to a stop only feet behind his pickup. Shifting the truck into park, he jumped out and without another thought ran inside the barn.

In the closest stall to the back door, a man lay on the ground, and Audrey, also on the ground, kicked him. She was bloody, and her hair matted to her skin. He noticed another woman in the stall. It was Pepper.

The man gained enough momentum to launch himself forward at Audrey. He landed on top of her and managed a punch right to the face before Gregory grabbed him and pulled him from her. When he did so, the man fell on top of Gregory.

Gregory rolled and knocked the man off of him, and was just about to start his assault when the sound of a shotgun ripped through the air.

There, he saw his father lowering his rifle toward the man. "The next shot goes right to your chest if you move," his father growled.

Gregory scrambled toward Audrey and kissed her softly. "Are you okay? Did he hurt you?"

"I'll be fine. I hurt like hell. But I'll be fine. But Pepper…"

Gregory looked up at his father who moved in closer to the man on the ground, and then Gregory got a look at the man.

Temper rose, and heat from his body moved to his head. He could feel the throbbing in his temple as he fisted his hand to his side. "You son-of-a-bitch!" Gregory moved to him and picked him up by his collar. Because his father was standing behind him with a shotgun, he was sure that Leo Frost wasn't about to move.

"Gregory, now let's…"

Gregory didn't hear anything else. He pulled back and punched Leo right in the face, knocking him back to the ground.

He watched as Audrey crawled to Pepper. "She needs help. She needs it quickly."

George Bishop pulled his phone from his pocket and threw it to her, never letting go of the rifle. Gregory listened as she called 911 and requested help.

"Tell me why you did this. Tell me why you hurt her and Audrey."

Leo's eyes, swelling from the punch that Gregory had landed, narrowed. "Actors are a dime a dozen. You happen to be worth more. But your damned goodness hinders everything. The only way I can get anything more from you is to sell your mistakes to the tabloids."

"Did you set that up? Did you have her be there in Las Vegas?"

Leo shook his head. "I didn't set that one. It just worked out to my benefit. Luckily you are stupid. And I wouldn't have gone after that new bimbo you hooked up with either, had Pepper not set her sights on her first."

His father moved in closer, this time resting the barrel of the gun on Leo's chest. "What did she do?"

"She planned to break into her house, even tried one night when you were there." He narrowed his eyes more. "I'm sure you remember what you were doing. She's the one that threw the brick through the front window. She wanted in on my plan."

Gregory knelt down next to the man he once called a friend. "And exactly what was your plan?"

He could have sworn Leo grinned. "I wanted more. Why the hell do you get all the glory? I'm the one who gets you the jobs. I'm the one that sets up everything. And I get a measly percent? Screw that. Do you know how much money I made selling the pictures of you and your ex with that stupid dog? Hell, all I had to do was throw her a new piece of meat, and she was all over it."

That stung, he thought, as he realized why his ex had disappeared. He didn't love that woman, and obviously, she was easily distracted from him. What kind of man did that to another man? One that devoted everything to him? It made Gregory sick.

"I'm pretty sure you're the stupid one here. Did you think you wouldn't get caught? Did you think I would really pay you to keep quiet? You both can go to jail. Your career is over."

Gregory could hear the sounds of the distant sirens. He looked toward Audrey, who tended to Pepper. Would any other woman tend to the woman who'd tried to destroy her life? He wasn't sure. All he knew was that Audrey was his perfect match. There was no question about it.

THE SHERIFF HAD DRIVEN AWAY with Leo Frost. If there was a charge Gregory could press against him, he would do it. Greed was such a horrible monster he thought as he walked into the house.

Audrey sat at the kitchen table, an ice pack pressed to her jaw.

"They want me to take you to the hospital," he said as he moved toward her. "They said that mark across your back needs to be tended to. They want to x-ray your jaw too."

Audrey groaned. "This isn't the first time I've been knocked to the ground. I'll be just fine."

"This was malice. No beating you ever took from brothers or cousins has been this bad. Or any fall from a tree for that matter," he teased.

Audrey smiled, then winced. "Fine. Take me to the hospital, but then can we head home?"

"Of course. I'll take you anywhere you want to go."

"You have a job to do. There will be nobody back home to get in my way anymore."

"I suppose I'm going to be out to get a new manager. It's hard to find someone you can trust," he quipped with a wink.

Audrey lowered the ice bag from her jaw and moved her head from side to side as if to loosen her muscles. "You should talk to Bethany. I'll bet she has some connections."

Gregory gave that some thought for a moment. He would talk to Bethany. He figured she'd make a fine manager, and he trusted any Walker implicitly.

EPILOGUE

Gregory sipped the champagne he'd been served, as he sat at the back of the reception hall. He wasn't sure why he was surprised at the grandeur of one of Lydia's receptions.

He'd enjoyed the party that she, Audrey, and Nichole had put together. Who knew a grand opening to a salon could have been so extravagant? That almost seemed like a lifetime ago now.

He didn't know he would miss Georgia quite as much as he had. Hawaii had been nice, but it had been nicer when Audrey was with him. She was much too busy to travel with him all the time though. After all, she now had three other stylists in her booming salon.

Until the premiere of the movie he filmed in Georgia, he was a free man between projects. That was until his new manager, Bethany, finished the deal she was working on for another film adaptation for one of Kent's books.

For the time being, Gregory was happy shacking up with Audrey in her little condo.

Black Sabbath stirred at his feet. It certainly wasn't usual to take a dog to a wedding, but a Walker wedding was a different story.

In the past six months, Gregory had been privy to a birthday party for Nichole's twins, two bachelor parties—one for Audrey's brother Jake, and the other for her cousin Dane— and now he sat in the back at the second of the weddings. Dane and Gia had opted for a small wedding, and then another in Lucca, Italy where Gia was from. Now he drank champagne at Jake and Missy's wedding. He'd never seen a wedding cake in the shape of racing tires, he marveled.

Though the dress that he had originally bought for Audrey hadn't gotten much more use, the Jimmy Choo shoes sure had.

As he finished the glass of champagne and absent-mindedly rubbed a hand over the back of the dog, he looked across the room at Audrey's aunt who expertly held both of her grandchildren. Chelsea and Susan had gone into labor only hours apart. Their daughters had been born only one day apart.

It made him miss his brother Scott's kids, but they had plans to visit. Even his sister had invited them to Japan to visit as well.

Audrey made her way across the dance floor in her shimmering bridesmaid's dress. The Jimmy Choo shoes were dangling from her fingers. She plopped down on Gregory's lap and pressed a warm kiss to his lips.

"Are you hiding back here?"

"Black Sabbath danced too much. He needed a break."

Audrey laughed as she laid her head on his shoulder. "This is a perfect life, isn't it? Family all around. Business is good. Your movies are wrapped up. Well, until your manager gets you a new one. Who knew everything would change that night you came through my door?"

"Are you needed for a few moments?" He asked as he rubbed a hand down her back. "I think Black Sabbath would like a little walk outside."

"I could use some fresh air."

They stood, and Black Sabbath got to his feet. Hand in hand they slid through the back door and walked down the sidewalk. The windows of the *Bridal Mecca* sparkled in the moonlight.

When they came to her salon, Gregory stopped. He looked through the window and then stepped back. "I think somebody left something in there."

"Oh dear," she said as she held out her hand and waited for him to hand her the keys to her salon, of which he now had a set. "Chances are it was somebody from the wedding party. If I hurry, I can get it back to them."

AUDREY PUSHED OPEN the door and Gregory and Black Sabbath followed. She moved to the bag that was on the table in the reception area and picked it up.

The bag was filled with tissue paper and a tag with her name on it. She pulled at the paper and underneath was a shoebox with the name Jimmy Choo across the side. Audrey pressed her lips together to keep her calm. Gregory was full of surprises.

She opened the box, and inside was a sparkly pair of white pearl shoes. When she turned to ask him why he had given her such a gift, she saw him down on one knee, the dog seated next to him. She pressed her fingers to her lips, and as her eyes began to well with tears, she noticed her sisters and her brothers all standing at the door.

"Gregory?" The name came out nearly inaudible.

In his hand, he held a ring box and the most beautiful diamond ring she had ever seen sparkled inside of it.

"I thought I'd better have them block the door. I didn't want you to run out," he said grinning widely. "The shoes will go with the ring, and the dress I will buy you. I thought this was the most appropriate place to do this. The very place I happened upon, and when I did, I found you. Audrey Walker, will you do me the honor of marrying me?" he asked as he nodded to the dog. "And Black Sabbath too, of course."

Audrey laughed through the tears. "Are you sure you want me? That's a lot of family to adopt when you marry someone," she informed him as she sniffed back tears and looked up to see her sisters doing the same.

"That's why I asked them first. I thought it would give me a fighting chance. So what do you say? Will you conquer this crazy world with me? Share your spirit with me, and the children that we will someday have? Oh, and the new dog. This one's going to want a friend."

Audrey moved to him as he stood. She wrapped her arms around his neck and pulled him in for a kiss that shook her to the core even more than the first one had. "I'm not sure you can handle the spirit that runs through this family. So, I will marry you so that you can try."

Gregory laughed as he stepped back, and took the ring from the box. He slid it on her finger, and then placed a kiss on her hand. "I promise you a lifetime of adventure. You will never regret this decision."

As Audrey looked down at the diamond that shimmered in the dark, she knew that she never would regret it. Her only regret was not having met him long before he'd come to Georgia and changed her life.

We hope you've enjoyed WALKER SPIRIT, book seven in the Walker Family series. Here is an excerpt from the next book, BEGINNINGS by Bernadette Marie.

BEGINNINGS

THE WALKER FAMILY SERIES ~ BOOK EIGHT

I t wasn't as if the wedding of his cousin to the movie star had been a surprise. The invitation had been sitting on Ben's kitchen counter for nearly a month. Then again, everything had been on the counter since he was taking his sweet time unpacking, since his move into the modular home he'd literally had dropped on his piece of the Walker Ranch land.

He'd have liked to have built his own home from the ground up, but where would he get the time?

A lot more responsibility had fallen on him since his brother, Eric, had become a father. It wasn't as if Eric completely blew off his responsibilities, but he'd sure rather spend time with his daughter.

Ben understood that. After all, one day he would like to have children too. He didn't see that happening anytime soon, though. It was hard to meet women when you lived 45 minutes away from the nearest city. Besides, he had never been good with women.

His mother had been trying to persuade him to take a date to his cousin's wedding, he thought, as he drove towards town. In his head, he made a list of five or six women he could ask, but when it came down to it, he knew he'd show up single.

His own reflection in the mirror caught his attention as he checked traffic behind him. His hair was a mess, and one more thing for his mother to harp on. He could hear her voice rattling his head. "You need a haircut before Audrey takes time off for her wedding."

Ben blew out a long, ragged breath. She'd been saying that for two weeks. Now, he was enroute to Audrey's new salon with the hopes that one of her employees could sneak him in for a necessary haircut.

He pulled up in front of the *Bridal Mecca,* the strip-mall his cousin Pearl and her sister-in-law Lydia owned. Nearly all the businesses were bridal related, except for his sister-in-law, Gia's, Italian gift shop. There was no denying that he was extremely proud of his family for what they had built. Sometimes he wished he had it in him to do something as big, but the truth was he much rather be around his family and the animals.

He parked his truck, and climbed out. The lights in the salon were still on, and he figured that was a good sign. His mother would probably kill him if he showed up to the wedding tomorrow looking like he did.

Just as he opened the front door, a small remote-controlled car jumped over the toe of his boot.

"Whoa! Did you see that?" The young voice came from a boy who darted from the back room and ran for the car. He picked it up, and looked up at Ben. "Who are you?"

"Ben. Who are you?"

The boy stood straight, as if she'd been trained to do so when meeting someone. "Zane. Did you come to get your hair cut?" he asked as he looked up at the mess atop Ben's head.

"Yeah."

Zane stood there studying him for another moment before he yelled, "Mom, there's a man out here who needs a haircut!"

Ben stood there, the door still open behind him, while he waited for the anonymous *Mom* to appear.

The moment that Nicole, Audrey's first employee, came from the back room, Ben's heart did a little flip in his chest. On her hip, she carried a little girl with hair color that matched her own dark brown hair.

"Hey, Ben. How are you? We were just packing up," she said as she let the little girl down to run off after Zane.

Ben shut the door behind him. "I didn't realize it was this late. I came to see if somebody could sneak me in for a haircut. The wedding is tomorrow and..."

A smile formed on her beautiful lips, and she pushed up her designer pink and black framed glasses. "The wedding is tomorrow and you forgot to get your hair cut?"

"Yeah, it's not looking too good."

Nicole laughed, and it made his heart flip yet again. "Let me settle these guys down, and then I'll get you in. We don't want someone to accidentally get a picture of you and putting in a magazine as a guest at the wedding of Audrey and Gregory Bishop if you don't look your very best," she teased.

The very thought that there would be photographers there to put the pictures into tabloids made Ben a bit uneasy. His cousin Bethany had been a movie star, of course he didn't see her that way anymore. He supposed, had she been around more often when she was a famous movie star, the entire family would have been exposed to such things as tabloids and reporters. She hadn't come back home until she had given up her movie career. It was her sister, Audrey, who was marrying Gregory Bishop, one of the leading stars in Hollywood. He thought it was interesting how a family who owned a ranch in Macon, Georgia had this many connections.

The noise around him drew him out of his own thoughts. Nicole gathered toys and set children in waiting room chairs. It was then he noticed there was one more boy, Zane's twin obviously, who must have just come out of hiding.

The three of them settled down with an iPad between them and the unmistakable sound of SpongeBob SquarePants.

Nicole let out a breath. "Okay. Are you ready?"

"Are these your kids?"

She gave all three a look. "Nah, I get lonely so I rent them."

The other little boy, whom he had yet to be introduced to, looked up at her. "Mom, why do you tell people that?"

She gave him a weak laugh. "Because my sense of humor is horrible and I think it's funny."

The little boy shook his head and looked back down at the iPad.

Nicole gave him a nod toward the shampoo bowl. "Yeah, they are mine. They're my whole world."

Ben sat down in the chair and reclined back, his head resting in the divot in the bowl. "I didn't know you had three kids. I've seen the pictures on your station, but I didn't know if those were nieces and nephews," he said as she turned on the water.

"I don't usually have them here. But tonight I was working late. You are not the only Walker man who was not prepared for this wedding tomorrow."

"Who else?"

She laughed again and it sent a tingle up his spine. "Sworn to secrecy."

He sat there quietly while the warm water ran over his head, and then she massaged shampoo into his hair. He was pretty sure he could fall asleep under the touch of her fingers.

Once she was done, she dried off his hair with the towel and led him to her station. Ben looked back at the kids quietly watching their iPad.

"They're pretty good," he said as he sat down in her chair.

Nicole draped the cape around him and fastened it in the back. "They are good kids. They had to do a lot of sitting around the last year waiting for me to get done working. I try to make it up to them."

"Well, if you ever need any help..."

Nicole laughed loudly as she ran a comb through his wet hair. "I'm sorry. I should never laugh when a man offers his help with children. Are you good with children?"

Then let his shoulders drop. "Honestly, I don't know. My brother's stepson is five now, I think. I get along with him. I also have two new nieces."

"I know. I've been around them, remember?"

That was right. How had he possibly forgotten? Probably the same way he'd forgotten he'd seen her with her children at weddings and parties over the last six months. That was his own fault. He seemed to get nervous and tongue-tied whenever she was around. Most of the time, he found himself hiding in the kitchen or outside with the stragglers at wedding receptions.

He watched her in the mirror as she began to cut his hair his hair. He figured they weren't too far apart in age, though she might have a few years on him. It was funny to think this beautiful woman had three well-behaved children. He knew she had moved to town six months ago, and she'd moved from Colorado. That was a big adventure as far as he was concerned. He, on the other hand, had only moved out of his parents' home. No wonder he didn't have a woman who would want to go to the wedding with him. When he thought of it, he sounded like a loser.

Nicole kept the conversation going as she cut his hair, and Ben wondered if he'd ever learn to loosen up around her.

"So who are you taking to the wedding?" she asked as she pulled her small set of clippers from a drawer.

"I'm going by myself."

"That surprises me. You're a good-looking guy."

Ben clasped his hands in his lap underneath the cape. "How about you? Who are you going with?"

Nicole turned around and looked at three children sitting with their heads pressed together. "Those are my gorgeous dates. But maybe you'll save me a dance?"

Ben wasn't sure he answered, as she took the cape and brushed the hair from his neck.

"You look perfect," she said giving him a wink. "I'll see you tomorrow then."

Then pulled his wallet from his back pocket. "How much do I owe you?"

She rested her hand atop his. "Just save me that dance."

While he stood there, more than likely with his mouth open, she folded up the cape, cleaned up her station, and began to gather up her children.

Ben slid his wallet back into his pocket. "Thanks. I'll make sure to save that dance, maybe a couple extras too," he said, without really thinking it through first.

He let himself out of the salon, and looked back inside as he closed the door. Nicole looked up at him, smiled, and gave him a wave as she tucked items into a bag while kids tugged at her to get her attention.

Ben wondered if his heart rate would slow down before he saw her tomorrow. He seemed to be a bit infatuated with her. What was he thinking? She was a beautiful woman, one with three kids and a missing husband. Chances were, all he'd ever get was a promised dance.

As he climbed into his truck and drove away, he realized that's all he had in him anyway. It all went back to the reason he didn't have a date for the wedding. He wasn't very good with women.

ABOUT THE AUTHOR

Bestselling Author Bernadette Marie is known for building families readers want to be part of. Her series *The Keller Family* has graced bestseller charts since its release in 2011. Since then she has authored and published over thirty books. The married mother of five sons promises romances with a *Happily Ever After always...*and says she can write it because she lives it.

Obsessed with writing since the age of 12, Bernadette Marie officially started her journey as an author in 2007 when she finalized a manuscript she'd been writing for 22 years, shelved it, and wrote 12 more books that year. In 2009 she was contracted with a small publisher in a deal that would eventually go bad. From that experience, she knew she could take control of her career and that's what she did.

A chronic entrepreneur since opening her first salon at the age of twenty, Bernadette Marie established her own publishing house in 2011, *5 Prince Publishing,* so that she could publish the books she liked to write and help make the dreams of other aspiring authors come true too. Believing there is a place for the fresh author's voice, she not only publishes but coaches others who wish to publish their work independently. Bernadette Marie is also the CEO of *Illumination Author Events and*

Services offering smaller intimate author/reader events as well as author services.

For more information

www.bernadettemarie.com
info@bernadettemarie.com